"Wait, Alex. You said to follow this chemistry to its logical conclusion. But marriage is a big step— are you sure you're ready for it? You have been a bachelor for an awful long time."

Saffron deliberately lowered her voice, a slight tremor to her tone.

"Marriage? Who mentioned marriage?" He let go of her and stepped back as if he had been stung.

"I'm sorry if I misunderstood," she said softly, acting for all she was worth. "But I'm afraid that's the only way you'll ever get me."

JACQUELINE BAIRD began writing as a hobby when her family objected to the smell of her oil painting, and immediately became hooked on romance. She loves traveling, and worked her way around the world from Europe to the Americas and Australia, returning to marry her teenage sweetheart. She lives in the north of England, and has two grown-up sons. She spends most weekends with husband, Jim, sailing their small boat.

Books by Jacqueline Baird

HARLEQUIN PRESENTS

Don't miss any of our special offers. Write to us at the following address for information on our newest releases.

Harlequin Reader Service
U.S.: 3010 Walden Ave., P.O. Box 1325, Buffalo, NY 14269
Canadian: P.O. Box 609, Fort Erie, Ont. L2A 5X3

Jacqueline Baird

A Devious Desire

Harlequin Books

**TORONTO • NEW YORK • LONDON
AMSTERDAM • PARIS • SYDNEY • HAMBURG
STOCKHOLM • ATHENS • TOKYO • MILAN
MADRID • WARSAW • BUDAPEST • AUCKLAND**

ISBN 0-373-11827-9

A DEVIOUS DESIRE

First North American Publication 1996.

CHAPTER ONE

SAFFRON flopped back down on the plastic chair at the roadside café and grinned at the elderly lady seated at the opposite side of the table. 'I've paid the bill and asked the proprietor to call us a taxi. It's half six and we have to be back on board by seven.'

'Don't fuss, child, and finish your wine.'

'Your wish is my command,' she quipped. 'But remember that is your third glass. Don't blame me if your arthritis plays up later on.' And with a wry smile tugging her wide mouth Saffron picked up her glass and sipped the sparkling wine. She hadn't the heart to deny Anna a few moments longer at the café in the ancient walled town of Rhodes. A café Anna had spent hours trying to find!

'What was so important about this particular place?' Saffron asked for the umpteenth time, but not really expecting an answer. Anna had been very secretive about the reason behind her search for this café, but Saffron wasn't complaining.

A month ago she had been working as a beauty and aromatherapist for a London agency that provided a personal service to clients in their own homes, and also to a few of the more enlightened city hospitals, when a request for a home visit from Anna Statis's doctor had arrived. The lady had had a fall and badly bruised her shoulder, which, combined with arthritis in her knee, had left her in a little difficulty with mobility. He had considered that aromatherapy might help her. Saffron was given the job. Ten days later she had a six-month contract as Anna's personal therapist, and for the past week they had been cruising the Greek Islands on the liner the *Pallas Corinthian*. Life could not be more perfect. Saffron sighed in contentment, and raised her glass to her lips.

They had just spent an enjoyable afternoon walking around Rhodes, discovering the Street of the Knights and marvelling at the inns that housed the Knights of St John. Then finally they had found this small bar, much to Anna's delight and Saffron's relief; she did not want the old lady overtired.

'My son was conceived here.'

'What?' Saffron jerked upright and swallowed the wine, almost choking with laughter. 'You're having me on. In a pavement café?' Her sparkling green eyes clashed with misty blue ones.

'It is true. I was a dancer on a cruise ship. Very daring for a well brought up English girl in my era. The ship visited Rhodes regularly and I met and fell in love with a handsome Greek, Nikos Statis, and in a room above this café my son Alexandros was conceived forty years ago this week.'

Saffron glanced at her employer, not sure whether to believe her. In her mid-sixties, her once blonde hair, now white, was swept up in a loose chignon, revealing the delicate features of a still beautiful face, but a sad, reminiscent smile hazed her blue eyes.

'And now you're back again. How romantic,' Saffron murmured. But privately she had her doubts. Within a week of taking up her live-in job as Anna's therapist she had watched in awe as the old lady had persuaded her doctor that what she needed to make a quick recovery was a cruise! Anna might look fragile, but she had an amazing ability to get her own way.

'Romantic! I thought so at the time,' Anna continued softly. 'But I was wrong—so wrong.'

Saffron was intrigued and, eager to hear more, prompted, 'Wrong...?'

'Some day I will tell you my life story. I feel the need to tell someone, and in the short time we have been together I feel closer to you than I have to anyone in years. Probably because you have been on your own and lonely most of your life and so have I.'

'But you have a son.' Anna was always talking about him, but he neglected the woman shamefully. As far as Saffron was aware he had never so much as called his mother since she had started working for Anna.

'Yes, true.'

Obviously they were not close. A typical selfish male, Saffron thought, but at that moment a taxi drew up at the kerb, and she knew any further revelations would have to wait.

Anna drained her glass and in a lightning mood change grinned. 'Finding this place today has helped me to lay some ghosts. But now we'd better make tracks, hmm?'

'Yes,' Saffron agreed and, standing up, she added with a smile, 'I'm glad we found your café. You do look more content.'

'Content! Yes, do you know I really think I am? Thank you, Saffy.'

With a tender glance at her boss, Saffron swung her shoulder-bag over her shoulder and gently put a hand under a frail elbow, helping Anna to her feet. She waited and watched as the other woman gave one last lingering look at the top floor of the building and was just about to help her into the car when to Saffron's astonishment someone yelled, 'Get the hell out of the way!' and grabbed the strap of her bag, hard fingers scraping her bare flesh.

Her hand slipped from Anna and she cried a warning. 'Look out! A thief!'

Years in an orphanage, and looking after herself for most of her life, along with classes in self-defence, had taught Saffron something, and with lightning reflexes her arm shot up, her finger and thumb nipping the front of her attacker's throat while her knee crashed up and into a very male groin. Spinning on her heel, she gently pushed Anna back into her seat. 'Don't worry, Anna, I've got it under control.'

Saffron shot her a worried glance, and was amazed to see that Anna was not in the least fazed by the unpleasant incident. In fact she was smiling, then chuckling, then laughing!

'It's not funny—we were nearly robbed.'

'Oh, Saffy, dear, if I ever had any doubt about your suitability for the job, I don't now!' Amid much laughter mingled with very masculine groans she went on, 'I have never seen anything so funny in my whole life.'

Saffron, adrenalin still pumping, had no idea how magnificent she looked. At five feet five, with her red-gold hair a wild tangle about her lovely face, and dressed in neat white tailored shorts, braless under a navy strapless tube-top, her green eyes flashing fire, she looked like some avenging Valkyrie.

'What is so funny?' she demanded, and then spared a glance for the man she had felled. 'This man was trying to attack us.' She could not see his face, but she could hear his moans. He was folded double and clutching a very private part of himself.

They had gathered quite a crowd, including the proprietor of the café, who asked, 'Shall I call the police?'

The police... Saffron hesitated. They had to be back on board soon; if they were delayed by the police they would miss the boat. She glanced at Anna, only to see the other woman wiping the tears of laughter from her eyes with one hand while waving the other frantically in the air as she got out over her amusement. 'No police, no police.'

'Then let's get in the taxi and go.' Saffron was suddenly conscious of the crowd and being the centre of attention and she did not like it. She hitched her bag more firmly on her shoulder and cast an uneasy glance at her assailant, who had dragged himself to the seat she had recently vacated, and she saw his face...

Night-black hair fell in tousled curls over a broad forehead; perfectly arched brows framed glittering black eyes. The nose was large and slightly hooked, the jaw square, and wide mouth completed the rugged features, but the lips were pulled back in a grimace of pain. Her gaze dropped to his broad shoulders; a plain white T-shirt clung lovingly to a broad chest, the faint trace of dark body hair showing through the fine fabric, and brief denim cut-offs exposed the considerable length of tanned muscular legs, also with a downy covering of black hair. He looked dangerously tough, and suddenly Saffron had serious doubts about what she had done. Her legs felt weak, and she was amazed at her own success in overpowering him. If she had got a good look at him before, she would never have tried...

Odd! He also looked vaguely familiar, but he couldn't be... Dismissing the uncomfortable thought, she said quickly, 'Come on, Anna; get in the taxi. We don't need to bother with his sort; the police will catch him soon enough.' She opened the car door and put her other hand under Anna's elbow, urging her up and into the taxi. She was desperate to get away. The man looked as if he was getting his wind back and Saffron did not want to be around when he did.

'No, no, Saffy, you don't understand,' Anna said, still chuckling. 'This is my son Alexandros. Alex.'

'What? Your son!' Incredulity widened her green eyes to their fullest extent. 'I don't believe you. He can't be...'

'But he is. Honestly...' Anna, finally controlling her amusement, answered seriously.

'Thank you, Mother. I'm glad you found my distress so hilariously funny.' A deep rich voice broke into the women's exchange.

Saffron felt as if she had been pole-axed, then her lips began to twitch in the beginnings of a smile as she thought that actually it was the man who was pole-axed, and by her! She knew it was completely the wrong time to find the situation amusing but she could not help it— a snort of laughter escaped her before she could control herself.

'And as for you, whoever you are,' the deep voice continued harshly, 'I would not laugh if I were you; if anyone is calling the police around here it will be me for your completely unwarranted attack upon my person.'

'Oh, for heaven's sake, Alex, listen to yourself! You sound like a pompous ass,' his mother responded, and, grabbing Saffron's arm, she added, 'I think you're right, dear; let's get in the taxi and go; we don't want to miss the boat.'

But their escape was not to be so easy. With a speed that belied his great size and his recent injury, Alex was on his feet and ushering his mother and Saffron into the back seat of the cab. Sliding in beside them, he then issued instructions to the taxi driver in Greek, and they were on their way.

'Now, Mother, perhaps you will tell me what you are doing with this red-headed devil——' he cast a venomous glance at Saffron who was squashed between them, and then looked past her to his mother '—on a cruise ship touring the islands.'

'Having a holiday,' Anna said bluntly. 'Saffy is my new companion—and before you say another word Dr Jenkins thoroughly approves.'

Saffron felt the dark eyes fixed on her, but she kept her head bent, hiding her face. After the excitement of the past half-hour, she was slowly beginning to realise just what she had done. Assaulted her employer's own son. So much for the job of a lifetime, she thought morosely. She had been counting on this six-month contract with all living expenses provided to boost her bank balance to the magical amount that would enable her to set up her own beauty clinic. She could see her dream disintegrating before her eyes. Burnt to ashes by the heat of anger that shimmered between the taxi's occupants.

Suddenly Alex aimed a torrent of rapid-fire Greek at Anna, and as if to punctuate his words he stretched a long arm along the back of the seat to touch his mother's shoulder. At the brush of his arm against the back of her neck Saffron almost jumped out of her skin, a tingling awareness making the small hairs on her neck stand on end. Immediately she was shockingly conscious of his powerful masculinity and bitterly resented the fact.

She had met his type before—hard and ruthless. Even his mother had hinted that they were not very close, and she was lonely. Now Saffron could understand why, given the autocratic way he had bundled them both into the taxi like so much unwanted baggage. 'Arrogant pig!' she thought, then to her horror realised that she had spoken out loud, and the full fury of glittering black eyes was turned on her red face.

'Woman, if you want to live to see tomorrow I suggest you keep your mouth shut. You have done quite enough harm already. Kidnapping Mother, attacking me... One more word and you will be in a Greek gaol so fast your feet won't touch the ground——'

'That's enough, Alex,' Anna cut in sternly. 'A taxi is not the place to argue, and in any case we have arrived.'

Alex, without another word, got out of the car and walked around the other side, opening the door for his mother. Saffron slid out on to the dock and glanced up at the cruise liner, then rather warily over the top of the taxi at the other two. As she watched she saw Alex smile and bend down to brush a light kiss on the top of Anna's head before paying the taxi driver then gently taking her arm and leading her up the gangway.

Saffron hesitated. Perhaps she was wrong. Maybe Alex did not neglect his mother. As she thought back to the scene at the café it struck her. For a woman who said she hardly saw her son, Anna had not been in the least surprised when he had suddenly appeared. In fact she had thought it a huge joke. Odd. Very odd...

A soft sigh fluttered past Saffron's lips. What did it matter? She had little doubt that in a very short time she was going to be out of a job. It would have been nice to finish the cruise but if the murderous expression on Alex Statis's face earlier was anything to go by she would probably be on the next flight out of Rhodes back to England.

But in that she was mistaken...

Once back on board she deemed it wise to give mother and son some time alone and grasped the chance to speak to a fellow traveller, a nice American gentleman who was travelling alone. She listened to him wax lyrical about the beauty of Lindos—the destination of the shipboard excursion that day—then slowly made her way to the cabin.

As soon as she walked in the door she immediately sensed the tension in the air. Anna was sitting in an armchair, her lovely face composed, her hands folded neatly in her lap, while Alex paced up and down the cabin like a caged tiger.

'Don't hurry, will you, Miss Martin?' He fixed her with piercing black eyes, and she shivered at the force of his anger.

'I wasn't aware there was any hurry,' she snapped back. 'After all, we are on the boat for three more days.'

'You are not.' Saffron's heart sank at his words. So she was to be sacked! But to her astonishment he continued, 'You are to pack for the pair of you, and be ready to leave as soon as possible. I will arrange with the captain to delay sailing until you are ready, but hurry—every extra minute over departure time is going to cost me dearly.'

'What?' Saffron wasn't sure she had heard him right. They were leaving the ship, but to go where? 'Where?' she exclaimed.

'My yacht. And I have no time for questions. Mama insists you fulfil the six-month contract; she seems to think you are invaluable to her.'

His eyes swept over her from the top of her red head, lingering for a moment too long on the proud thrust of her breasts beneath the brief top she wore, and on down to her narrow waist, slim hips and long legs, then back to her face, his expression saying it all. He couldn't see why! Then, with two lithe strides, he was beside her.

Her hands curled into fists as she fought down the instinctive urge to push him away; he was much too close. She stiffened, banishing the blush that rose to her cheeks with a mighty effort of self-control. There was something about the man that threatened her in ways she didn't understand. Sexually, she freely admitted, but it was more than that. On some deeper, darker level he threatened her. She knew it instinctively, but not why. She raised her eyes to his harsh face and searched the rough-hewn features with the growing conviction that somehow—somewhere—she knew him. Then suddenly his words penetrated her puzzled mind.

'I have met your kind before, and I am not so sure you're of any value,' he drawled cynically. 'More likely a costly mistake.'

Saffron gasped in outrage at his comment, and raised her hand to slap the swine's face. But he caught her hand in his and continued insultingly, 'However, against my better judgement I have agreed to allow you to stay for my mother's sake.'

Saffron felt the electric shock the length of her arm as his strong fingers tightened on hers deliberately. 'Smile,' he hissed, and added loudly for Anna's benefit, 'We have a deal, Saffron. Shake on it.' And she was forced to comply with the social nicety before he finally let go of her hand.

She was still reeling when he bent his head and murmured, as he brushed past her through the open door, 'But don't think I've forgotten what happened earlier; I'm going to make you pay, you green-eyed witch,' and left, slamming the door behind him.

Anger and fear mingled in her eyes. The arrogant devil! How dared he threaten her? For two pins she would walk out now, but, catching Anna's expression, she fought down the impulse. The appeal in the older woman's eyes was unmistakable.

'I apologise for my son; he can be rather domineering, I know, but he does have my best interest at heart. You will still come with me, won't you? I need you.'

'I'm not sure it's a good idea,' Saffron said drily. 'Your son and I are obviously not going to get on, especially after I nearly crippled him.' A fleeting smile curved her mouth as she remembered his discomfort earlier.

'That wasn't your fault; I'm sure he won't hold it against you, Saffy. In any case the yacht is huge and if I know Alex we will rarely see him; he always brings one of his women with him, if not more than one, and of course the *family*.' She frowned, adding cryptically, 'That is the main reason I wanted to come on a public cruise. It's much more fun with strangers around.'

Saffron's heart sank. How could a son treat his mother so cavalierly? Take her on holiday, then leave her to her own devices while he enjoyed himself with his latest sex object? She was sure that was all women meant to such an aggressively macho man as Alex and his own mother had more or less confirmed it.

'But the doctor did say you had to have no stress. Maybe it would be better for you if you told your son the truth. You fell and got a nasty shock, but soon you will be as good as new.' Anna had sworn both her doctor and Saffron to secrecy over her accident, insisting that she did not want her son to know and fuss over her. Personally Saffron thought it was way past time her son fussed over her, instead of leaving her in London all the time while he apparently based himself in Greece when he wasn't jetting around the world. 'I'm sure if he knew he would stay with you, and you won't need me.'

'You don't understand, dear. I can't tell Alex; I know what he will say—that I'm too old to live on my own. He will insist on my giving up my London home and staying with the family. I would hate that. I like—I need my independence. Please say you will stay...'

Saffron sighed inwardly. She could not desert her charge, however much she might dislike the poor woman's son. But 'poor woman' was not really accurate. She smiled to herself. Even the mighty Alex Statis had bowed to his mother's demand and allowed Saffron to stay. Anna, despite her delicate old lady act, was obviously a wily old bird.

'Yes, of course,' she answered a touch wryly, and moved to the wardrobe, adding, 'I'd better start packing.'

* * *

Saffron turned restlessly in the bed, and pushed the light satin cover down to her waist. But she knew it was not the heat keeping her awake—the yacht was fully air-conditioned—nor the low throbbing of its powerful engine as it ploughed through the Aegean Sea in the middle of the night. It was the intervention of the frightening, sinister figure of Alex Statis in her life.

With an efficiency she could only marvel at he had whisked her and Anna away from the cruise ship and, after a brief taxi ride, into a waiting helicopter; by ten o'clock the same evening, to her amazement, the helicopter had landed on a helipad on the top of a luxurious ocean-going yacht, anchored off the Greek mainland.

With a minimum of fuss a very correct steward had shown Saffron to her cabin on the top deck, and what a cabin! A large circular bed in a mahogany-panelled room with a matching *en suite*, the bathroom and toiletries all sparkling white with brass and mahogany trim. Anna's quarters were even more luxurious, with a private sitting-room.

Saffron had tried to quiz her boss while unpacking, but for some reason the older woman had not been very forthcoming. However, while Saffron had gently brushed Anna's hair, before settling her for the night, she'd begun to talk.

'I guess I was being irresponsible to go off on my own that way—at least, Alex thinks so,' she murmured softly, almost to herself, and then, looking in the mirror, she fixed Saffron with pleading blue eyes. 'But you understand, don't you, dear?'

Saffron didn't, not one bit; her head was reeling at the events of the evening. Dinner had been an informal buffet, not because of the lateness of the hour—Greeks were used to eating late—but in deference to the fragile health of her charge, she was sure. After the meal Alex had taken one look at his mother and then told Saffron to see the lady to bed. Saffron had been only too happy to comply; for the last few hours she had been all too conscious of Alex's eyes following her every move, studying her as if she were something the cat had dragged in, and the feeling had been unsettling to say the least.

She smiled at Anna's reflection in the mirror. 'Not really,' she confessed simply.

'No, I suppose not. It was an old lady's fantasy to re-create the past. The *Pallas Corinthian* was the boat I worked on, you see, the one I later found out Nikos, my husband, owned...'

'You mean you got me to book a cruise on your own shipping line?' Saffron had wondered, when Anna had asked her to book the cruise, why she had insisted on the one particular ship. Now she knew.

'Not exactly. Alex is in charge of the business, has been for ages, and he sold the liner to another company years ago. He has no time for sentiment. That's why I couldn't tell him what I wanted to do. But I'm glad we had our little holiday, Saffy; seeing Rhodes and the café today was enough, and thank you again, dear, for pandering to a sentimental old fool.'

Instinctively Saffron put down the brush and gave Anna a hug. 'I don't think you're an old fool; I think you're wonderful. And now do you want me to massage your shoulder before bed or not?'

'No, not tonight. I'm tired enough to go straight to sleep.' Rising, she touched Saffron's cheek. 'You're a good girl to put up with me, but there is one little thing I would like you to do.'

'Yes.' Saffron realised that in the past few weeks she had grown to really care for Anna and, arrogant son apart, she would do anything for her.

'Please don't mention to Alex why I wanted a beauty therapist as well as a masseuse. I would hate him to know I can't even lift my arm high enough to comb my own hair. He is an astute man, and would soon guess there was something more wrong with me than arthritis, and it would only worry him.'

Personally Saffron thought it was about time the globe-trotting swine did worry about his mother, but not by a flicker of an eyelash did she reveal her dislike of the man; instead she promised to say nothing.

Tossing and turning in the luxurious bed, Saffron tried to tell herself that nothing much had changed from this morning. They were still cruising but simply on a private yacht. So why did she have this weird feeling of foreboding? It didn't make sense. She still had her job, in a week or two she and Anna would return to Anna's comfortable mews house in the heart of London and Saffron would rarely, if ever, see Alex Statis again. All she had to do was keep her mouth shut and out of his way; that shouldn't be too hard; she was just the hired help after all...

She closed her eyes and once more tried to sleep, but the vivid image of Alex leaning against the door-frame as she'd walked by him to follow Anna to her cabin seemed to be imprinted on her pupils. Casually elegant, his black hair swept back from his broad forehead, grey wings curling around his ears betraying his thirty-nine years, and a wide, sensual mouth that had hissed cynically as she'd passed him, 'You can leave now. But I haven't forgotten I owe you.' That parting shot lingered threateningly in her mind.

Her eyes flashed open. 'You can leave now,' he had said, and something niggled at the back of her brain, a sense of *déjà vu*. Had she met him before? No, it wasn't possible; her mind must be playing tricks, or—perhaps the most likely explanation—she must have seen a photograph of him in his mother's house. Yes, that was it—of course. And, closing her eyes once more, she finally fell into a troubled sleep where a tall, dark man stalked her dreams...

A knock on the door broke into her restless sleep and, slowly opening her eyes, she yawned widely.

'Coffee, madam,' she heard the steward announce, and responded.

'Come in.' Hauling herself up into a sitting position, she blinked drowsily, wondering if Anna was awake yet. Then it hit her, the events of the previous evening, and her eyes widened in horror on the approaching man, a gasp of outrage escaping her. 'You...'

Alex, dressed in a brief white towelling robe belted loosely around his waist, revealing a wide expanse of hair-roughened chest and inordinately long, muscular legs, strolled to the bedside, a tray bearing a coffee-jug and cup on it in his strong hands. 'Good morning, Saffron.'

'G-g-get out of my room,' she stuttered. The man wasn't conventionally handsome, but he possessed a lethal attraction few women could resist, herself included. His tanned skin, the early morning stubble darkening his jaw gave him the rakish appearance of a swashbuckling pirate.

'Now is that any way to greet your employer? Especially when he is delivering you sustenance.'

'You are not my employer,' she retorted, but his remark had reminded her of her duties. 'But if you get out of my cabin I can dress and go and see Anna,' she said, suddenly wide awake, and wary. She had no idea how lovely she looked, her red-gold hair tumbling in disarray around her shoulders, one long strand with a will of its own curving around the fullness of her breast, the skimpy spaghetti-strapped cotton nightie she was wearing barely covering her high, firm breasts.

'You're not a morning person... Pity, because you look absolutely delectable.'

How dared he flirt with her? Saffron's angry eyes flew to his face and she was horrified to realise that his gaze was fixed rather lower on her body. Grabbing the luxurious satin sheet, she pulled it up to her chin. Just in time, as Alex sat down on the side of the bed. He was much too close, the bedroom was much too intimate, and he had no right to be here.

'Will you get out?' she cried, her temper rising.

'Don't look so terrified. You must have had dozens of men in your bedroom, a girl as beautiful as you.'

She had never had any man in her bedroom, and she was damned sure she wasn't about to start with this overpoweringly arrogant specimen of the male sex. 'Out,' she snapped, indicating the door with her free hand.

'Don't flatter yourself, girl,' Alex drawled cynically, his dark eyes sliding insultingly over her flushed face and rumpled hair. 'I only want to talk before you see Mama. Why else would I wake you at seven in the morning?' he asked mockingly.

Saffron could do nothing about the blush that suffused her whole body.

Alex slowly shook his head, one dark brow arching sardonically. 'What a naughty mind you have, Saffron.'

The man delighted in teasing her, but she had promised to try and get along with him, so, ignoring his comment, she turned to where he had placed the tray on the table beside the bed and filled a cup with coffee. She took her time adding milk, before she dared turn back to face him.

'Tell me, why Saffron? I always thought it was a spice. Are you spicy?' he queried, a wicked glint in his dark eyes.

She slanted him a glance from beneath thick lashes then quickly looked down at the cup in her hand and took a long swallow of the hot coffee, before responding curtly, ignoring his innuendo, 'Saffron is a plant that when dried yields a deep yellow, orangey dye. When I was born my parents took one look at my ginger hair and called me Saffron.'

A large hand reached out and picked up the loose curl that framed her breast. Alex twisted it around his long fingers, his knuckles brushing the tip of her breast. 'Your hair is not ginger, it is gold, red, blonde, a collection of colours creating a living flame.'

Her breast hardened at the brief touch and embarrassment at her instant reaction brought hot blood to her cheeks. Saffron knew that Alex was aware of her response and suddenly she felt helpless, as if she had lost control of the situation. Yesterday she had been a mature, efficient professional doing her job to the best of her ability. In the past twelve hours her life had quickly become entwined with this sophisticated man and his jet-set lifestyle, and she wasn't sure she liked it. She pulled her head back, freeing her hair from his far too familiar fingers; and quickly lowered her eyes, afraid of the predatory look on Alex's harsh face.

But the following view was even more disturbing as her gaze dropped to where his robe fell apart, revealing a tanned muscular leg in stark contrast to the white towelling. A startling erotic image flashed through her mind as he moved slightly, his taut thigh pressing against her leg, only the satin sheet preventing their naked flesh touching: Alex, naked and golden brown all over, reaching for her, his deep brown eyes smouldering with passion...

'Coffee. Good.'

Horrified at her wayward thoughts, Saffron tore her gaze away from his legs and, shocked by her sexy fantasy, kept her head lowered to hide her blushes. She mumbled, 'Yes,' then breathed deeply and exhaled slowly. Her reaction to Alex Statis was getting ridiculous. What on earth was happening to her? She prided herself on her self-control but she had an awful premonition that around this man she would have to fight for every ounce.

'Cabin OK?' he asked.

He knew very well it was the height of luxury; he was deliberately goading her, but she would not rise to the bait. 'What do you want, Mr Statis?' she demanded firmly, pleased at the even tenor of her voice.

'It is not so much what I want but what you want, Miss Martin.' All trace of teasing was gone. His eyes, hard and dark as jet, caught hers. 'My mother is a wealthy woman. I don't know who persuaded whom to go on a holiday cruise which was totally unnecessary in the circumstances.'

'I didn't...'

'Maybe you're telling the truth. Mama can be very devious,' he said drily.

Anna devious! Well, maybe a little, Saffron admitted honestly, but compared to this man Anna was innocence personified, and she listened in mounting anger as Alex continued.

'I've checked with her doctor and apparently it is all above board. My mother likes you, she tells me you are good at your job, and I know to my cost——' his lips thinned in a tight grimace '—you are more than capable of looking after yourself and her. But what worries me is where you learnt such talent, and why you needed to. So take this as a warning if you have any notion of fleecing my mother, or getting involved with any more of her madcap plans; I advise you to forget it—understand?' He got to his feet, his dark eyes boring down into hers, a threat explicit in the black depths. 'I will leave you to enjoy your coffee—oh, yes, and welcome aboard.'

Saffron had never been so insulted. The nerve of the man! Madcap plans indeed! And as if she would cheat an old lady. The temper that went with her red hair ex-

ploded, and she threw the half-full cup of coffee straight
at him. The cup bounced off his chest, spilling coffee
all over him.

'Why, you...' Two strong hands caught her upper arms
and dragged her off the bed and against his hard body.
She was suspended in mid-air, her feet dangling inches
from the floor, but she did not have time to dwell on
her predicament as a dark head swooped, Alex's mouth
capturing hers in a brutal grinding kiss that drove the
breath from her body. She tried to struggle and felt
herself falling...

CHAPTER TWO

SAFFRON fell back on the bed and felt the full weight of his huge body follow down on top of her; she tried to lift her knee, but Alex wasn't the sort of man to be caught twice. His naked thigh pushed firmly between her legs, and as she tried to claw at his face his hands caught hers and pinned them either side of her head.

'You damned hellcat,' he swore. 'Yesterday you got lucky. For the first time in twenty-odd years you caught me off guard. But it was also your last, sweetheart. It is time someone taught you a lesson, and I am just the man to do it.' His deep brown eyes had darkened to black and the flame leaping in their depths sent fear scudding through Saffron's body.

'Says who——?' Her last word was all but swallowed by his mouth once more closing over hers, his tongue gaining entry to the moist interior with devastating results. Suddenly she was conscious of his naked thigh between her legs, her short nightie rucked up somewhere round her waist; his towelling robe had fallen open and their lower bodies were naked flesh on flesh... Her breasts pressed against his muscular chest, hardened with inexplicable need and straining against the fine cotton of her nightgown.

To Saffron's dismay, heat fierce and totally unexpected flooded through her veins. Her heartbeat accelerated like a rocket, and the kiss she had fought so furiously turned into a passionate seduction of her senses. She was aware of his powerful, virile body

24

through every pore in her skin. His heavy thighs moved restlessly against her slender limbs, and something else...

Well, I certainly did not injure the man yesterday, she thought wildly, just as Alex's mouth left hers, and she burst into terrified hysterical laughter.

'What the hell...?' His dark head reared back and he looked down into her flushed, laughing face. He let go of her abruptly and stood up.

Whether he recognised that it was fear more than humour that had brought on her hysterical reaction Saffron didn't know; she only knew that, with a savage glance at where she lay tumbled on the bed, he snarled, 'Cover yourself, woman; I'm not caught that easily,' and pulled the sheet up over her.

Caught? What did he mean? She gazed up at the dark figure towering over her, and all trace of hysterical humour left her. He was virtually naked; his robe, hanging loosely off his broad shoulders, hid nothing of his magnificent body, or his obvious state of sexual arousal. Her earlier fantasy was fulfilled. His powerful body was tanned all over, except for a pale strip across his lean hips! Mesmerised by the stark beauty of his virile form, she could not look away...

'Remember, you've been warned,' Alex said coldly as unselfconsciously he folded the robe over his chest and knotted the belt around his waist. 'Now I suggest you do what you were supposedly hired for and look after Mother.' And with that he strode out of the room, slamming the door behind him.

Saffron lay where he had left her, completely shell-shocked. Nothing in her life so far had prepared her for such a lightning attack on her senses. Her body still pulsed with unfamiliar heat, her breasts felt heavy, the tips aching for she knew not what, and the lingering scent of Alex hovered in the air around her, seducing her even in his absence.

It was incredible—no, impossible, she told herself. She did not like the man, and yet for an instant she had wanted him in a shockingly sexual way. She who could count the men she had kissed on the fingers of one hand!

Slowly, as her breathing reverted to normal, she justified her reaction. It must have been a mental apparition; her response was not real, just a figment of her imagination. She was twenty-five years old and knew herself well enough to realise she was not a sexual person. Two unfortunate events in her teenage years had quickly squashed any real interest in the male sex.

At the age of ten she had lost her parents in a car crash and, left alone in the world, she'd been placed in an orphanage. It was quite nice, the staff friendly, but it could never make up for the loss of her home in Surrey and her parents. She had been thirteen, her body beginning to develop, when one of the older boys had caught her and forced her to the ground, his hands grabbing at her breasts. But Eve, her friend, had stopped him.

Saffron sighed and swung her legs off the bed. A soft film of moisture glazed her eyes as she stood up, remembering the past. Eve, two years older than Saffron, had been her best friend at the orphanage. Even after she'd left, she'd still called back occasionally to see Saffron. Eve's untimely death not many months ago had affected Saffron deeply; she still wasn't over it. She brushed the moisture from her eyes and headed for the *en suite*.

Memories were best left where they belonged—in the past. She stepped out of her nightie and into the shower; turning the tap on full force, she tossed her head back and let the reviving water wash over her.

The sensible thing to do was to pack in her job as soon as the boat docked and return to England. She would miss Anna, but common sense told her that the older woman would have no problem getting someone else to fill her role, and if she stayed she would have a problem with Alex Statis. He was a powerful, dangerous man, and he made no secret of the fact that he thought she was after something from his mother. It would be difficult; she had given up her room in the apartment she had shared with two others, Tom and Vera, and they had been quite happy to see her go as they had decided to marry, and quite naturally preferred to have the place to themselves. She supposed she could stay in a hotel or hostel until she found somewhere else, but it would certainly cut into her business fund, she realised sadly.

Then she recalled once more Eve's last message to her.

You have it all, Saffron—the looks, the character and the expertise to make it on your own. Not like me. I was born a loser. Promise me, Saffron, you won't let some bastard of a man get at you. Stick to your dream. Start your own business, be your own boss. Do it for me. You show them.

Squaring her shoulders, a new light of determination in her lovely green eyes, she turned off the water and stepped out of the shower. Wrapping a large fluffy towel around her slender body, she walked back into the bedroom. She would not allow Mr Statis to frighten her out of her job. Anna had employed her. Anna was happy with the arrangement, and in any case once they got back to London she would not have to see the man. But her salary for the next few months would be enough to fulfil her dream. Ten minutes later, neatly dressed in navy shorts and a plain white T-shirt, she opened the door of Anna's suite.

'Oh, you're awake!' Saffron smiled at her employer, sitting propped up in bed, her glance going to the tray beside her. 'And already at the coffee, I see,' she chided gently; if Anna had one weakness it was that she drank far too much coffee.

'Yes, my dear. I received the same service as you, apparently. Alex delivered it.'

Saffron felt the colour rise in her face. Anna certainly had not been attacked by the great brute as she had! Walking to the dressing-table, she busied herself with the case that contained her oils and other supplies. Trying to hide her blush, she said, 'Would you like me to order breakfast or would you prefer a shower and massage?'

'The massage, but make it quick. I have been instructed by Alex to meet him on the deck for breakfast at nine-thirty, and I don't dare argue. I have already wasted three days of his time, he informed me.'

'Wasted!' Saffron's temper rose at the comment. 'Surely it's his own fault? We were perfectly all right on the *Pallas Corinthian*. This was his idea.' She flung out an arm, gesturing around the luxurious room.

'Well, not exactly. I have a confession to make.'

Saffron spun round to stare at her charge.

'You see, dear, we always cruise in June for a week or so. But with Alex being in Australia and not sure when he was coming back I decided I wanted to cruise on my own... well, with you. The poor boy arrived in London last weekend and didn't know where I was and so he spent three days tracking us down, instead of working. Ordinarily I would have joined the yacht at the weekend along with Alex and the rest of the relatives.'

'If that's so, why are we moving now?' Saffron glanced out of the window at the vast expanse of clear sunlit water. 'We could have waited in port for the other guests and your son could have stayed at work.'

'That's my fault. I insisted we set sail straight away because I was frightened that with a couple of days in port you might change your mind and go back to England. I know what a pain my son can be, and I didn't

want to lose you. This way you can't get off the boat
and I've told Alex he has got to make friends with you.'

'Why, you conniving lady,' Saffron opined, with a wry
shake of her red head.

'Yes, but you know my secret. In any case no one can
do my hair or make-up as well as you. Not even me
when I was fit,' Anna said with blunt honesty.

An hour later Saffron put the finishing touches to
Anna's hair and then followed her along the passageway
down the companionway, through the staterooms and
through large glass doors to the poop deck where Alex
was waiting for them.

It had been dark last night when they had arrived, but
Saffron had been awed by the luxury of the cabins, the
elegant main lounge and equally stunning dining-room,
but the deck was something else again. Under a plain
white awning were arranged three plump-cushioned long
sofas covered in William Morris shades of blue and green
printed cotton satin, a couple of over-stuffed armchairs
and one large low table plus a handful of smaller ones
discreetly stacked beside one of the potted vine trees that
dotted the area. Beyond the seating area, on the open
deck, was a circular swimming-pool. Through the
sparkling water Saffron saw the outline of dolphins patterned in the tiles; the effect was as if they were swimming
in the pool and completely magical. Around the pool
was scattered a dozen sun-loungers, and a few more
tables with gaily patterned beach umbrellas in the centre.

How the other half live! Saffron thought, bemused.
She had realised Anna was wealthy, but it was slowly
dawning on her that Alex Statis must be extremely rich.
No wonder he was worried about his mother being ripped
off by some unscrupulous companion. But it still gave
him no right to suspect her, she thought grimly. He didn't
know her, and was never likely to. She was way below
his social circle and she knew it.

Subdued, Saffron sat down in one of the armchairs, avoiding looking at where Alex lounged elegantly on a sofa opposite. But to her surprise breakfast was a pleasant meal. The same steward who had shown her to her cabin the previous evening placed a wide variety of cereals, croissants, bread and accompanying confections on the large table, along with jugs of coffee, tea and various fruit juices, before asking if anyone wanted a hot meal.

The conversation was general. Saffron made an occasional comment but after a while she left mother and son to do most of the talking, content to admire her surroundings. It was early June, and the hot morning sun sparkled and danced on the deep blue sea, dazzling on the brilliant white of the boat. Paradise must be a lot like this, Saffron mused as she spread thick honey on a second warm croissant. Heaven help her weight if she kept eating like this...

'Is that all right with you, Saffron?'

She jumped at the sound of her name, her glance flashing between the other two. She felt that some comment was expected of her, but hadn't a clue what had been said.

'Tell her again, Alex,' Anna said with a grin.

Saffron reluctantly looked across at Alex. He was lounging casually back on the sofa, with his long legs stretched out in front of him. His hard, dangerously masculine body was briefly clad in a sleeveless black T-shirt that moulded his broad, muscular chest in loving detail. A pair of white shorts exposed his long legs, tanned to a golden bronze and rippling with muscles. He was all male, all-powerful, and he made her head spin...

'We will be arriving in Mykonos in a couple of hours. Mother wanted to see the island again, but she does not

feel up to going ashore in the tender.' He hesitated and
Saffron raised her eyes to his questioningly.

'She suggested I take you.' His sensuous mouth curved
mockingly, his dark eyes raking suggestively over her
slender frame. Saffron felt the colour rise in her face at
his *double entendre*, before he added slowly, deliberately, 'For a few hours.'

The lazy smile, the long body stretched out only feet
from her were having a totally alien effect on her. She
opened her mouth to say no, but was horrified at the
odd constriction in her throat. She swallowed hard.

'Yes, of course she will,' Anna answered for her.
'Mykonos is not to be missed.'

'I don't know,' Saffron heard herself murmur; she
knew intuitively that being alone with Alex Statis rep-
resented a danger she was not sure she could handle.

'Of course you will, dear,' Anna insisted.

Saffron glanced across at Alex; the amusement in his
eyes was obvious; he knew she wanted to say no, and
was daring her to... 'Yes, that would be lovely,' she
heard herself gush, and missed the flicker of cynicism
in Alex's dark eyes.

'Good. Well, if you will excuse me, ladies, I have work
to do.' Rising to his feet, Alex smiled gently at his mother.
'Round one to you, Mama.'

His austere features relaxed in a genuine smile that
took years off his age and, though his comment puzzled
Saffron for a brief second, she saw the man behind the
ruthless mask. She sucked in her breath, her green eyes
wide with wonder; he looked almost beautiful. But as
he glanced briefly at her the tenderness vanished, to be
replaced by a glittering predatory glow that turned his
deep brown eyes almost golden.

'I'm looking forward to showing you Mykonos. I want
to see your reaction to the place.'

A frisson of some nameless emotion slid down her spine. Fear! No. Anticipation of a day out, Saffron told herself sternly, nothing more! She refused to acknowledge her inexplicable violent attraction to Alex. 'I'm sure it will be delightful,' she offered with a cool smile, but had to turn her head away to stare at the sea. In her mind's eye the sight of him standing so tall and broad, scantily clad in shorts and shirt, was doing something very peculiar to her breathing.

Saffron stood leaning on the ship's rail, Anna beside her, as they watched the crew lower the gangway and the boat that in a few minutes would take Alex and herself ashore. The island of Mykonos looked everything Anna had told her as they had lounged around the boat all morning, relaxing and chatting.

The yacht had dropped anchor in the bay of Mykonos Town, and the view was spectacular—sparkling white houses, the blue-topped domes of the small churches the place was famous for dotted among them, along with the impressive row of windmills, six marching in a line along the horizon. Tearing her gaze away from the beauty before her, Saffron tried once more to persuade Anna to accompany them.

'I'll help you down into the boat, Anna. You will be all right, I promise. It seems a terrible shame for you to miss going ashore.'

'Rubbish! I can see all I want from here. Don't forget, Saffy, I have been here countless times.'

'Well, if you're sure.'

'Positive. I want you and Alex to forget about me and don't come back until you have seen the sunset from Little Venice.'

Before Saffron could reply Alex was at her side. She glanced up at him and her heart jumped. He had changed from the morning into a pair of navy shorts and a navy and white patterned silk shirt, and he looked devastatingly attractive.

'Ready, Saffron?' He drawled her name like a caress, sending tingles down her spine. 'Got your bathing suit?' he demanded, his dark eyes gleaming knowingly down into hers. He knew exactly how he affected her and obviously found it amusing.

'Yes,' she said frostily, swinging her beach bag, and would have preceded him down the gangway but a hand on her arms stopped her.

'Gentlemen first in this instance, then if you fall I am in front of you to prevent a hasty descent into the sea,' he explained, before releasing her arm and stepping on to the ladder.

The small boat reached the shore in minutes. A hire car was waiting for them and moments later they were speeding out of the town and into the countryside.

'I thought we were going to see the town,' Saffron prompted, a bit miffed that Alex appeared to have a different idea.

'We will later, first we will drive around the island, go for a swim maybe. There are some magnificent beaches. One or two nude ones if you prefer.' He shot her a wicked sidelong glance.

'No way,' she snapped back.

'Why not? It will be nothing we haven't seen before after this morning.'

A telling tide of red suffused her face as for a second she saw in her mind's eye Alex as he had been that morning in her room—almost naked.

Alex laughed out loud at her obvious discomfiture. 'OK, you win; bathing suits it is.'

It was like a day out of time for Saffron. After that one bit of teasing in the car Alex set out to be charming company, and Saffron found her antagonism vanishing in a puff of smoke.

They lunched on succulent fish on a bed of rice and fresh vegetables, at a small café alongside an almost deserted beach. Afterwards they lingered over their wine, and eventually strolled along the beach.

She found Alex an informative and amusing conversationalist as he told her something of the island's history. Apparently not that long ago it had been just another tiny Greek island inhabited by shepherds and fishermen. But the stylised form of building all white with the distinctive blue touches had been seen as so picturesque that a crafty local had decided they should cash in on the tourist trade. Now it was extremely popular with all the cruise liners, but was never overrun, simply because the bigger ships could not dock. The only way ashore was by tender.

By mid-afternoon the sun was much stronger in the sky and Alex suggested that they rest for a while. From the small duffel bag he was carrying he withdrew a towel and spread it on the golden sand, and Saffron followed suit, cautiously laying her own towel a foot away from his.

'Spoilsport,' he murmured as casually he slipped out of his clothes and stood before her clad only in tiny black swimming-trunks that left little to the imagination.

Saffron gulped and dragged her gaze away from such a blatant display of sheer masculine perfection. He might be nearly forty, she thought, but not a spare inch of flesh marred his tall, muscular frame; he had the body of a man in his prime, and she was beginning to wonder at the wisdom of being alone with him.

'Race you to the water,' Alex challenged, and she had to look up at him.

'You go—I'll catch you up.' She needed a couple of minutes alone to still her erratically beating heart. She watched as with a casual nod he turned and began to run down to where the turquoise water met the silvery sand. He was as enticing from the rear as from the front, his broad tanned back tapering down to gorgeous lean hips and long, muscular legs. God! What was she thinking of? In a rush she slipped off her plain denim skirt and the neat short-sleeved shirt she had worn over her swimsuit.

She glanced down at herself, and wondered if the suit had been such a good idea. She had bought it for the cruise, thinking it was more conservative than a bikini, but now she had grave doubts. In jade-green, it was a simple figure-hugging Lycra suit with high cut-away legs almost to her waist, strapless and slashed straight across her breasts. Suddenly she saw just how provocative it was. How come she had never noticed before? she groaned silently, but it was too late to do anything about it now, and, taking a deep breath, she ran down and into the water. She could see Alex's head bobbing in the distance; he was a magnificent swimmer, but she had a sneaky suspicion that he was the kind of man who would do everything magnificently.

Saffron did not bother to try and compete; she could swim but was no great shakes, so she stayed near the shallows and floated for a while, enjoying the soothing stroke of the water against her sun-warmed flesh. Occasionally she glanced at Alex, who appeared to be heading determinedly towards an outcrop of rock that to Saffron looked miles away. He swam with a rhythmic determination that she could only marvel at. Slowly, with a sigh—it wasn't disappointment at Alex ignoring her, she told herself firmly—she made her way back to shore.

Collapsing flat on her back on the towel, allowing the sun to dry her, she closed her eyes. The hustle of the past two days, the food and wine at lunch, and the warmth of the sun all combined to make her fall asleep.

'Saffron!' She woke up with a start, for a moment completely disorientated and wondering where she was.

Alex was leaning over her, his body damp, drops of water
glistening on the dark hair of his chest and taut, flat
belly. He frowned down at her. 'Don't you know it is
the height of stupidity to fall asleep in the sun?' His
hand reached out and with one finger he traced the soft
curve of her breasts revealed by the straight bodice of
her swimsuit. 'This flesh is far too fair and tender—you
will burn,' he opined huskily.

'Alex,' she murmured dazedly; his touch was doing
unreal things to her pulse-rate. She wanted to ask him
if he'd enjoyed his marathon swim, but he was quite
openly studying the soft swell of her breasts, his finger
tugging lightly on the taut fabric, lowering it slightly.
She shivered as his finger dipped down almost to the
crest of one breast. She knew she should object, but had
not the will to stop him, hypnotised by the sensual gleam
in his eyes and his throatily voiced comment.

'So silky and voluptuous. A perfect combination.'

He smelt of sun and sea and sky and a lingering masculine scent that was all his own. He moved, and she
felt the length of his leg move over her thigh, entrapping
her slender limbs, as his dark head lowered, blocking
out the sun.

'Saffron…' he rasped. 'You drive me mad.' And deep
down inside her Saffron felt something spring to life—
a matching madness. Perhaps…

She knew she should move, get away, but instead her
tongue licked nervously over her suddenly dry lips as she
anticipated his kiss. The hot brush of his lips over hers
made her gasp; his hand cupped the round fullness of
her breast and gently squeezed as his mouth moved more
determinedly against hers, his tongue thrusting inside,
arousing a response in her that she had never experienced with any man before. She felt his instant reaction,
his length hard against her lower body, and he broke the
kiss with a groan of frustration.

There was no 'perhaps' about it, she thought helplessly as, wide-eyed and trembling, she stared up at him.
He looked dark and threatening, his eyes narrowing as
they scanned the pale oval of her face.

'God, Mama has surpassed herself this time!' he exclaimed almost angrily. 'How old are you, Saffron—
nineteen? Twenty?' His fingers deftly readjusted the top
of her bathing suit, and his leg slid off her body so that
he was lying on his side. Propped on one elbow, he stared
down at her with an expression of disgust twisting his
harsh features. 'I must be crazy,' he muttered.

Finally finding her voice, Saffron responded in what
she hoped was a steady tone. 'Flattered though I am, I
happen to be twenty-five, almost twenty-six.' And why
he should mention his mother she had no idea...

'Thank God for that. I don't seduce young girls.'

'And you're not seducing me.' Saffron sat up abruptly, shoving at Alex's chest so that he fell on to his
back. 'I think it's time we left here; I've had enough sun
for one day,' she babbled as it sank into her bemused
mind just where his question about her age was leading.

A strong hand curved around her shoulder as she tried
to stand up. 'Wait, Saffron. I know we started off on
the wrong foot yesterday, though you have to admit that
was not solely my fault. But we are two consenting
adults; surely we can be sensible about this?'

Saffron turned her head to gaze down at Alex. His
deep brown eyes were fixed on her face, the residue of
passion still lingering in their depths. 'Sensible?' she
queried.

'Yes. I want you, more than I have wanted a woman
in years.' He cast a rueful glance down his long body,
and Saffron's eyes followed his and then quickly looked
away. The man had no shame, she thought furiously;
he was quite blatantly aroused. 'It's been a long time
since a woman has got me this way so easily, and I think

we should explore the possibilities. I know you want me—you tremble every time I touch you. So how about it?'

It was the very matter-of-fact way in which he stated his case that infuriated Saffron. Springing to her feet, she looked down at where Alex lay. He looked like some basking killer shark, about ready to devour its prey. And she was it... Snatching up her towel, she shook it over his supine form, covering him in sand. 'In your dreams, buster!' she scoffed and, grabbing her clothes, she stormed off down the beach, his deep laughter ringing in her ears.

Of course five minutes later she had to walk back, but at least she was fully clothed, she told herself. Just let him try anything else and she would flatten him, she vowed.

'Perhaps I didn't put that in quite the most flattering of terms,' Alex began as he pulled on his shorts and slipped his shirt over his broad shoulders.

'I am not interested in any of your terms, Mr Statis,' Saffron responded stonily. 'Now, can we leave? I did want to see the town of Mykonos—that's what we came ashore for. Not your sleazy suggestions.'

Alex shot her a quizzical glance. '"The lady doth protest too much, methinks." You wanted sex as much as I did, only you're not prepared to admit it,' he told her casually as he caught her hand. She tried to pull free, but Alex, with one glance and a dry, 'Don't be childish,' quelled her revolt and side by side they walked back to the car.

Saffron was determined not to speak to him again, and on the drive back she kept a stony silence. Eventually, when they arrived in the town, Alex turned to face her and said quietly, 'OK, I apologise. Truce, pax, friends...' and held out his hand. 'I promise, no more teasing.'

Saffron felt the colour scorch her cheeks. What a fool she had been; twice in one day she had melted in his arms, while to him it had been a huge joke. Calmly she put her hand in his and agreed, and she told herself she was not disappointed. Of course Alex could not seriously want a girl like her. His own mother had told her he had women galore.

Soon the charm of the town, and an apparently reformed friendly Alex, swept the earlier episode on the beach to the back of her mind. No one could fail to be delighted with the tiny streets, and the windmills that even Alex didn't know the reason for. Finally, as the sun began to sink lower in the sky, he led her to Little Venice. The buildings were right on the edge of the sea and the upper storeys hung out over the water in marvellous timber balconies. They walked up a tiny winding flight of stairs to a delightful bar which Alex insisted was the best on the island, with a perfect view of the sunset and classical music in the background. Sitting by the window at a tiny table for two, Saffron had never experienced anything so romantic.

'What would you like to drink, Saffron?' Alex asked quietly; it was as if even the great Alex Statis was affected by the atmosphere.

Saffron turned glowing green eyes on his rugged face. 'Anything—you choose. This is just perfect.' She could not contain her delight and, stretching out her hand, she touched his arm fleetingly. 'Thank you for bringing me here.'

'The pleasure is all mine.' Alex smiled back, and for an instant Saffron could only stare; his dark brown eyes gleamed with a rare tender warmth, and the effect on her senses was electric.

The waiter arrived with a whisky and soda for Alex and some fabulous red concoction for Saffron, with an umbrella and a sparkler burning in the glass.

'Cheers,' she toasted Alex as she removed the sparkler and took a sip. 'I said "anything" but I didn't expect to get a flaming potion.'

They laughed together, and then in unspoken accord turned their attention to the view from the balcony, as the sun turned to brilliant scarlet and slowly sank towards the horizon.

The music changed and Saffron recognised it immediately; the opera was a secret passion of hers. 'Rossini—my favourite composer!' she exclaimed. 'The overture to *The Thieving Magpie*, I think.'

'You like his overtures?' Alex's dark eyes lingered over her fine features, taking note of the mass of hair that rivalled the sunset in its colour.

'Yes, I adore them,' she said, slightly uneasy at his unwavering scrutiny. 'I have quite a collection.'

'Yes, I can see why. You're a romantic and as impetuous, pulsing and sometimes as abandoned as Rossini's music. It's all there in your cat's eyes and your magnificent hair—your passionate nature.'

Saffron was about to deny his reading of her character angrily, then realised that what Alex had said about the music was true. Did her love of Rossini disguise an impulsive passionate nature? The thought worried her... She was here on a Greek island with a man she hardly knew... And, lost in her own thoughts, she barely heard his cynically murmured comment.

'Let's hope the title does not accurately reflect you as well.'

She glanced warily across at Alex; his dark eyes caught and held hers. For a long moment the sunset, the surroundings disappeared; they were the only two people in the universe, and something deep and compelling seemed to flow between them.

'You agree with me,' Alex husked softly, and she did not think he was talking only about the music.

She forced herself to look away and, picking up her glass, drained it, making no response. She couldn't...she was terrified. After one day with Alex, a few kisses and now a glance and a simple observation on her choice of music, the man had made her recognise her own sexuality in a way she had never considered before. She had always thought of herself as a passionless sort of girl, if not frigid. Sex and romance played no part in her life. With a sense of shock she realised that the be-all and end-all of her life for years had been her burning ambition to succeed on her own. She had no close friends, except perhaps Eve, who was now dead...

She turned and gazed at the sea; the Statis yacht, aptly named *Lion Lore*, rode at anchor and as she watched the coloured lights from prow to stern flashed on, as the sun sank below the horizon in majestic glory, turning the sea blood-red.

'You must visit the outdoor opera in Verona; it is an experience not to be missed.' His hand covered hers on the table. 'Will you let me take you, Saffron?' he asked in that throaty, sexy voice of his, his thumb teasingly stroking her palm.

In that second she realised she wanted to say yes! But she knew he was asking for a lot more than an evening at the opera and, snatching her hand from his, she jumped to her feet. 'It's time we left. Anna will need me.'

'She's not the only one,' Alex taunted softly as he led her out into the balmy night air. Stopping at the edge of the water, he turned her to face him, linking his hands loosely around her waist.

Saffron tensed. Why did his words sound like a threat, she wondered, when his every look and touch promised her delights she could only guess at, and secretly longed for...?

'Funny. For a girl with a passion for overtures...' he bent and brushed the top of her head with the lightest of kisses '...you are very slow on picking up on them.' His dark eyes smiled teasingly down at her.

Saffron grinned, her tension vanishing. 'God, that was a terrible pun, Alex!'

'It worked—it made you smile.' And, holding hands, they made their way back to the yacht.

CHAPTER THREE

DINNER was again an informal affair; Anna had arranged for a hot and cold buffet to be served, unsure at what time Alex and Saffron would return.

Once more in the company of the older woman, Saffron sighed with relief, and the tension of the afternoon and her complete capitulation to Alex's sexual charm faded to the back of her mind as the three of them partook of a leisurely meal on the rear deck beneath the star-studded canopy of the night sky.

Saffron sipped her wine and cast a speculative glance beneath her thick lashes at Alex. He and his mother were discussing some people they knew and Saffron was quite happy to let the conversation wash over her as she secretly studied him. He wasn't really handsome—his features were too hard-cut and there was a certain ruthless hauteur about him that said, Watcher beware!—and yet he fascinated her as no other man she had ever met had.

Why was that? Why did she find herself wondering what it would be like to lose her virginity to a potent, sensual man like Alex Statis? Under her dress she felt her breasts go suddenly heavy; she trembled and folded her arms defensively across her chest, sitting straighter in the chair and fighting down the colour rising in her throat.

Why did he affect her so intimately? And, more important, why did she think she knew him? she asked herself for the hundredth time. He was way outside her sphere of experience, and yet there was something...! He was dressed as casually as usual in cream trousers and a blue knit polo shirt, his bare feet slipped into a pair of navy loafers, and yet the feeling of leashed power just below the surface was blatantly apparent. She'd bet he was a dynamic businessman, and she wondered just what kind of business he was in. Anna had told her the cruise line was now only a tiny part of Alex's business interests. He kept it going in deference to his late father, but he had expanded into a host of other projects.

'Sorry, ladies, but I have work to do.' Saffron was jolted back to awareness by the sound of Alex's voice. Startled, she looked up as he rose to his full height— well over six feet—and for a moment his dark gaze settled on her upturned face.

'Don't keep Mama up too late, will you, Saffron? We have guests arriving tomorrow.'

'Hmmph!' Anna's inelegant snort prevented Saffron from answering. 'It's time you got yourself a decent wife and presented me with a few grandchildren, instead of fooling around.'

'I might surprise you and do just that, Mother.' He held Saffron's gaze even as he responded to Anna. 'What do you think, Saffron? Would I make a good husband?' he asked with mocking amusement.

'I wouldn't know; I don't know you,' she said coolly and, turning her head, she caught the oddest look on Anna's face.

'Then I'll have to make sure you do,' Alex murmured, before moving to drop a brief kiss on the top of Anna's head and adding, 'You promised to behave yourself, Mama, so make sure you do.'

Saffron's puzzled glance slid between the two of them. 'What was that about?' she asked when Alex had gone. 'You always behave yourself.'

'Yes...well...you haven't seen the guests yet,' Anna replied with dry irony, and Saffron could get no more out of the woman, though she did try as she saw her safely to bed.

By seven o'clock the following evening Saffron was beginning to see what Anna had meant. The boat had docked earlier in the day at an exclusive marina on the Athenian riviera some half an hour's drive from the centre of Athens. She hadn't seen Alex since breakfast that morning, when to her astonishment, on leaving the table, he had kissed his mother as usual and then bestowed a brief kiss on her—Saffron's—softly parted lips as well, with the muttered comment, 'As set-ups go, you're the best yet.'

Blushing fiery red, Saffron had glanced at Anna to see her smiling like a Cheshire cat. 'What was that about?' she'd asked suspiciously.

'Forget it, Saffy; Alex is a law unto himself.'

Forgetting had not been so easy, but they had seen nothing more of him until a couple of hours ago, when three long black limousines had drawn up and he'd appeared with his guests.

'Give me your arm, dear, and let's get the greetings over with,' Anna had commanded as the party had trooped up the gangway.

'You don't sound very enthusiastic.' Saffron cast a worried glance at her employer as she took the older woman's arm and walked along to the foredeck and main reception area.

'I'm not,' Anna whispered in an aside before turning to the woman approaching her with a social smile. The woman was obviously Greek, and about the same age as Anna, but still very attractive.

'Katherina, how lovely to see you.' Kisses on both cheeks were exchanged and then Anna turned to a younger woman. 'And Maria—how nice. And who is your friend—or is it your friend, Alex?' She eyed her son, who brought up the rear of the group with another, older man.

'Allow me to introduce Sylvia, who for the past three years has been the very efficient director of our health and leisure chain.'

Saffron's head jerked round in surprise. So Alex owned a string of health clubs. Now why should that bother her? But it did. There was something niggling at the back of her mind, and if she could just remember ... But she did not have the chance as she was swept into a flurry of introductions.

Sylvia, the only English member of the party, was about thirty and stunningly attractive, with black hair, dark eyes, a perfect figure and face, and a smile that would have floored Casanova himself. She dismissed Saffron with a contemptuous glance once she realised she was only a companion. As did Katherina and her daughter Maria. The older man, Spiros, was apparently Katherina's husband.

Saffron shot a worried glance at Anna, who seemed to have gone very quiet among this crowd of confident relatives, and, edging her way to her side, she asked, 'Are you all right?'

Alex caught her whispered question and responded for his mother. 'Of course she is; she is with her family.' But Saffron wasn't so sure. And now, Saffron having just finished massaging Anna with a reviving mixture of aromatherapy oils, the pair of them were relaxing for a few minutes over a very English pot of tea, delivered by the steward a few minutes earlier.

'So what do you think of the family?' Anna asked with a cynicism that Saffron had never seen in the other woman before. 'You can be honest; I won't mind.'

'Well, I...I don't really know them; I mean, first impressions can be...' She was digging herself into a pit, but she was no good at lying. 'They're very Greek...'

Thankfully Anna's light laugh stopped her babbling. 'Exactly. Do you know, dear, sometimes I even forget my son is half English? He has such a Greek outlook on family. He insists every year that the relatives holiday together, and he has no idea of the agony it is for me.'

'What's the matter? Don't you get on with them?' Perhaps it was because she was English, but Saffron dismissed that notion immediately. The Greeks were very friendly on the whole, and had a particular liking for the English. No, something else was bothering Anna.

The older lady replaced her teacup on the small table, and dramatically let her head drop back against the soft cushions of the sofa. Then she looked at Saffron, her blue eyes serious.

'You remember on Rhodes when I showed you the café and I said I would tell you my life story one day? Today is the time, I think.'

'You don't need to.' Saffron was worried by the strange quality in Anna's voice. But, as if she had never heard her, Anna continued.

'I must; like all Greek tragedies it needs telling. My husband was an honourable man and he married me because I was pregnant. I loved him, and was happy. His elder brother was married to Katherina and lived in New York. My son was twelve years old when they first came back to stay with us. I saw my husband look at Katherina and I knew they were more than friends. At a party held in their honour she told me quite openly that my husband had always loved her, that she married his older brother because he was wealthier at the time, but she could get my husband at the snap of her fingers.'

'My God! That's awful.'

'Worse! She was right. I faced my husband with it and he admitted he had known her before his brother but he swore it was over between them years ago. I tried to believe him. His brother and family went back to

America, holiday over... Alex went to school in England and for the next six years we carried on as before, except I knew I had never been first choice with my husband.' Anna's blue eyes burnt with a brilliant intensity on Saffron's shocked face.

'He must have loved you——' Saffron began, but was cut off.

'Katherina and her husband returned when Alex was eighteen and she brought her daughter with her—we even holidayed together in England. And then a few weeks later her husband died and she became the grieving widow, and of course stayed with us, as is the Greek way. After a few months of having the woman share my house, I gave my husband an ultimatum. Alex was at university in England by this time and we had bought a house in London. I told my husband I was staying in London, and he had to decide either to get my sister-in-law and her daughter out of our home or get a divorce. I could not live with the situation. I had been in London two months when I got a call from Heathrow airport. He had arrived and wanted to talk. But, as in the best Greek tragedies, he was killed in a car crash on the way from the airport.'

'My God!' Saffron exclaimed, horrified, but she could not help noticing a glint of mischief in Anna's blue eyes.

'What could I do? I couldn't tell my son his father had been going to divorce me and marry his aunt; I didn't want to disillusion him about his father. Consequently my only son cannot understand why I'm not crazy about my Greek relations, and it drove quite a wedge between us.

'Ironically Katherina did set up in a villa in Athens just weeks after the funeral, but I stayed in London and Alex chose to spend most of his time in Greece. He dropped out of university and took over the business. Katherina married again five years ago, and my relationship with Alex has improved quite a lot over the past few years. I visit the villa on the island of Serendipidos every year. Actually it's my island; his father left the property to me. But now you can see why this annual cruise is not my favourite holiday.'

Saffron had never heard anything so appalling. For Anna to entertain year after year the woman she thought her husband had loved. If it was true; Anna was a great one for romancing, Saffron qualified to herself. But still, the stress it must create in the poor woman... 'But why on earth don't you tell your son? Surely it must be better than...?'

'No. Much as I love him he is more Greek than a true Greek—family is everything to him. At eighteen I could not disillusion him, and now it does not bother me that much.'

If the man weren't such an insensitive clod, Saffron thought privately, he would have realised himself years ago how his own mother felt. 'I still think you should have it out with him.'

'No—no way, child. I wouldn't have told you if I'd thought it would upset you.' She sat up straight, her quavering voice suddenly remarkably firm and strong. 'Just be sure you make me as beautiful as is humanly possible this evening. We eat in the dining-room at nine. I'm going to miss our casual buffet meals on the deck.' And, rising, she crossed to the dressing-table and sat down again. 'Come on, dear. Do your best; I want to outshine Katherina.'

And she did. Anna looked as beautiful as Saffron could contrive. With her long hair swept up into an elegant chignon, diamonds glittering at her ears and throat, and a classic designer-label full-length soft blue silk crêpe de Chine dress, cleverly cut to enhance Anna's still youthfully slim figure, she looked like the lovely lady she was.

Saffron had dressed with care in her one formal gown, a second-hand purchase from a small shop she knew in London. The Ralph Lauren design was a simple black sheath with black embroidery around the bodice and hem. It fitted her slender figure like a glove, and a thigh-high split enabled her to walk freely. The neckline slashed diagonally across her breast to leave one arm and shoulder bare. Her long red hair was swept up on top of her head in a mass of curls, a few stray tendrils curling around her face and the nape of her neck. She never wore much make-up but tonight she had gone all out, eyeshadow, mascara, blusher, the lot, and she knew she looked good.

With Saffron firmly supporting Anna, her hand under the older woman's elbow, they entered the dining-room together—late! But on purpose. Anna had not wanted to have to sit and sip pre-dinner drinks with the rest of the clan.

Alex was standing near the top of the table deep in discussion with his aunt and Sylvia and two men Saffron had never seen before. His dark head shot up as they entered, and he smiled across the width of the room.

'So glad you could join us, Mother; we were beginning to wonder.' His dark eyes flashed to Saffron and widened slightly before deliberately raking her from head to foot, a derisory smile curving his firm mouth. Saffron knew he was doing it on purpose and fought down the blush that threatened to overwhelm her.

'Charming, and no doubt time-consuming,' he drawled silkily. 'But if the job of looking after Mother as well as yourself is too much for you, Miss Martin, you only have to say.'

'Not at all, Mr Statis,' she snapped back. Gone was the teasing friendship of the past two days and his use of her surname put her firmly in her place, she thought cynically. A servant! But how dared he be so sarcastic with his own mother? she fumed, and was still fuming as Alex curtly introduced the two new arrivals. She had heard the helicopter earlier but had thought nothing of it.

Alex's PA was a tall blond Englishman in his late twenties called James. The other man, the company accountant, was much older, a Greek named Andreas. It made the party up to nine, and Saffron gave an inward sigh of relief; as the odd one out, she could sink into the background, do her job, and be ignored. But it didn't work out that way.

They took their seats around the large rectangular dining-table. Alex, of course, was at the head, his mother on his right hand and Sylvia on his left; next to Anna was Andreas and then Katherina and her husband while next to Sylvia was Maria and then James and lastly Saffron.

'We seem to be one man short,' Spiros chuckled.

'One good one is worth a dozen others,' Sylvia simpered, with a flirtatious look at Alex as she curved her red-tipped fingers around his arm.

Saffron could not help the contemptuous curve of her full lips as she saw the little scene enacted before her. Now she understood his reversal to her surname. His girlfriend had arrived and he did not want Saffron spilling the beans about his amorous flirtation with her.

She watched as Alex, looking stunning in a white dinner-suit, patted the hand on his arm and said, 'I'll take that as a compliment, Sylvia, darling.' His dark eyes lifted and caught Saffron's derisory glance and for second something flicked in the deep brown depths, but was quickly squashed as his cousin Maria spurted out a torrent of Greek.

Saffron took little interest in the conversation—she could not speak a word of the language anyway—so she was reduced to twiddling the cutlery through her slender fingers to still the nervousness in her stomach. She wished the meal were over with and she could leave. High society held no appeal for her, and there was something about Alex in a tailored white jacket as opposed to his usual casual clothes that she found irrationally threatening. So she was surprised when she looked up from the table and found all eyes on her, as though awaiting her comment.

Anna leapt into the silence. 'Maria was bemoaning the fact that her cabin is on this deck when usually she has your cabin. Alex was explaining that the four state cabins are occupied, Katherina and Spiros in one and Alex in the main cabin and naturally I need you next to me.'

'There is no need to explain, Mama; the matter is settled,' Alex said curtly, and Saffron felt her anger rise again at his abrupt treatment of both his mother and herself, completely ignoring the fact that he had defended her against his cousin.

Luckily the steward served the first course and in the ensuing chatter the matter was dropped. But it wasn't an easy meal. James made no secret of the fact that he found Saffron attractive and when he discovered that she lived in London and liked to wander around the London art galleries in her free time they got into a long discussion about the National Gallery, only to be interrupted by Alex.

'James?' Saffron glanced down the table, her green eyes clashing with Alex's suspicious brooding gaze, which quickly shifted to the man beside her. 'You are not here to seduce my mother's companion, but to work. Kindly remember that.'

Silence! A giggle from Maria broke the tense moment but Saffron felt her face turn scarlet. As for James, he turned astonished eyes on his employer and like a true English gentleman responded, 'My intentions towards

Saffron, or any other woman for that matter, are always strictly honourable.' He then spoilt his gallant reply somewhat by adding ruefully, 'If one values one's health in the present dangerous sexual climate, they have to be.' The ensuing laughter set the meal back on course and Saffron sighed with relief yet again, sure that the worst was over, but it was not...

The first course, a light pâté, was delicious; the next, lobster, with all the accompanying sauces, was perfection. But for the rest of meal Saffron never looked once at Alex, though she was aware of him in a way she had never experienced before. The deep resonance of his voice, his occasional laughter grated on her over-sensitive nerves. She'd never felt such an instant attraction to anyone. So why him? She wasn't sure she even liked the man, and bitterly resented his peculiar effect upon her, making it impossible for her to enjoy the sumptuous meal.

His deliberate sexual teasing of the previous day and her shocking reaction to it still rankled. He was so damn sure of himself! It was obvious that he had been making fun of her, filling in time until today, and the arrival of the lovely Sylvia. She noted that it had been Maria, not Sylvia, who had complained about her cabin—probably because Sylvia knew she would be sharing with her boss.

'Isn't that so, Saffron?' Alex's distinctive drawl cut in on her musing. He was back to calling her by her Christian name. Was she supposed to be honoured? she thought sourly. She looked up and saw once again that all eyes were on her.

'Yes, Saffron, do tell us,' Sylvia demanded. 'I can't believe anyone could get the better of Alex.' And she smiled, but Saffron, looking at the beautiful face, saw the spite in the hard eyes.

She had no idea what they were talking about, but help came from an unexpected source: Spiros.

'Did you really mistake him for a thief?' he asked, and she guessed what he was referring to.

Deliberately replacing her fork on her plate, she faced Alex down the length of the table. She could see the amusement sparkling in the depths of his brown eyes, and it enraged her.

'I wouldn't necessarily call it a mistake,' she opined with dry sarcasm, holding his gaze and delighting in the flash of anger in his dark eyes, 'but yes, I caught him by the throat and kneed him in the groin.' She said it with relish, and, pointedly turning her gaze on Sylvia, added, 'I'm sure the ladies in his life will have nothing to worry about—I doubt he suffered any permanent damage.'

Spiros's shout of laughter broke the tension. 'Damn! I wish I could have seen it—the great Alexandros brought to his knees by a slip of a girl.'

Everyone joined in with a comment and Saffron stroked one up for her then quietly withdrew from the conversation—or tried to, but James appeared to have other ideas. She had half expected him to ignore her after Alex's earlier comment, but with brave disregard for his employer he did no such thing, but continued to include her in the conversation at every opportunity, much to Saffron's rising embarrassment. She could feel Alex's dark eyes on her, watching her like a hawk.

Later, sharing a sofa with Anna and sipping coffee on the canopied deck, she was congratulating herself on having got Anna and herself through the evening reasonably well when to her horror Katherina began reminiscing. Saffron was convinced that the woman was doing it deliberately.

'It seems strange that Alex is the only male of the family left. Do you remember, Anna, when our first husbands were alive they were such loving brothers? And, incredible as it seems, it is seven years since I lost my own brother. All relatively young men, and so much sadness, and yet here we are, still a family.'

What a bitch! Saffron thought, casting a worried sidelong glance at Anna, but surprisingly she was smiling. What courage Anna had to put a brave face on something that, true or untrue, was still obviously hurtful.

Without a second thought Saffron got to her feet.

'Excuse me, everyone, but it has been a long day.' She saw Alex's head snap round to where she stood. 'Coming, Anna? It's getting late, and I have to massage your shoulder.'

'What?' Blue-eyed astonishment was quickly masked with a gentle, 'Yes, dear, of course.'

Saffron helped Anna to her feet.

'Shoulder?' Alex queried, his dark eyes spearing Saffron's with speculative scrutiny. 'I understood the arthritis was confined to Mama's knee.'

Saffron could have kicked herself; she had not been thinking clearly or she would not have made such a mistake. 'Yes—yes, it is, but...'

Anna came to her rescue.

'It's not important, Alex, simply a touch of rheumatism in my shoulder, and Saffy has the most soothing hands; I exploit her talent shockingly. If you will all excuse me I am tired.'

'I'll see you to your cabin, Mama.'

Saffron followed behind mother and son, up the stairs to the door of Anna's stateroom, and hesitated as the couple in front were talking.

'Is there something you're not telling me, Mother?' Alex asked quietly, a gentle arm around Anna's shoulder. 'I know how secretive you can be, but you know I love you and I only have your best interests at heart.'

Saffron was surprised by the wealth of caring in Alex's eyes as he watched his mother. Perhaps Anna should tell him the truth about her accident; this caring Alex might just possibly understand. But with his next words the illusion was shattered.

'Heaven knows as a family we see very little of each other—two or three times a year at most.'

'I know, darling, but you know me; I like London and the others don't.' Anna raised her hand and stroked his rough cheek in a gentle caress. 'Goodnight, son,' she murmured before opening the cabin door and walking inside.

Saffron moved to follow, but was stopped by a large, strong hand grasping her upper arm.

'Just a moment, Saffron.'

Reluctantly she halted. He was so close that she could smell the clean, tangy fragrance of his cologne, and the door shutting behind Anna seemed to leave the pair of them cocooned in the dimly lit passageway. 'What do you want?' she managed to ask levelly.

'You, Saffron,' he murmured sexily, and deep down inside her she felt her body's treacherous response and did nothing to evade his lowering head; she could almost taste his kiss. But instead he said, his deep voice close to her ear, 'But I can wait...' his warm breath touched her cheek '...until I discover exactly what you and Mama are up to.'

She trembled as his breath caressed her skin. She had felt desire before, but never anything like this... Yet she knew Alex was not serious. He was back to his sexual teasing of yesterday, and she had almost succumbed again. Stiffening her spine, she responded flatly, 'I have no idea what you mean. Now if you will excuse me Anna needs me.' And with her free hand she found the door-handle and turned it.

'So do I. Oh, so do I!' Alex husked, and with a swift bite on her earlobe that sent shivers down her spine he slowly relinquished her arm, his long fingers sliding down the slender length to her hand; his thumb stroked over her palm and his husky chuckle was enough for Saffron to snatch her hand away.

'Go tease Sylvia,' she grated between clenched teeth. He was not making a fool of her again. 'She will appreciate it—you're two of a kind.'

'Maybe!' His eyes narrowed on her flushed face. 'But don't make the mistake of thinking you and James are two of a kind. I will not allow it.'

His arrogance was incredible, she thought angrily, but was in no mood to argue. Hadn't she decided to get through this holiday with the least possible aggravation? She needed the money and as long as she remembered that and kept out of Alex's way she would succeed. Pushing open the door, she slipped into Anna's cabin, without a word, and closed the door behind her.

Anna was sitting at the dressing-table mirror, but turned as Saffron entered, a worried frown marring her gentle face. 'Do you think Alex is getting suspicious about my accident?' she asked immediately.

'No, of course not. He has probably just decided to keep a closer eye on you.' After neglecting you for months on end, Saffron added silently, but didn't say it, though she wanted to.

The next few days were a mixture of heaven and hell for Saffron. The yacht sailed majestically on through clear blue waters, the sun continuing to shine with the temperate heat of early summer that was just about perfect. They cruised around the group of islands known as the Cyclades from the island of Kíthnos to Sérifos, Sífnos, Kímolos and Páros.

Saffron did her best to avoid Alex, and Anna helped by insisting that they breakfast in her cabin. Saffron used her fair skin as an excuse not to join the rest of them around the pool for morning coffee. Instead she took to creeping out at seven in the morning and enjoying the pool by herself. But on the third morning that was also ended as the tall, dark figure of Alex appeared, his broad, muscular frame virtually naked except for black swimming-trunks.

Saffron gulped and almost swallowed half the pool when she first clapped eyes on him, but worse was to follow. His bronzed body executed a perfect dive into the water with an elegance that belied his huge frame, then surfaced where Saffron was holding on to the side of the pool. His brown eyes searched her face with an intensity that made her tremble. He lifted his hand to where her usually riotous curls were plastered to her head, and said, 'I know you from somewhere. We have met before, I'm sure of it.'

'That old line...' she snorted, but was stunned to re-alise that he was only vocalising what she herself had been thinking since the first time she saw him at Rhodes.

'Maybe we were soul mates in another life,' he mur-mured, his hand stroking over her head and down to her throat, 'and the desire has lingered on.'

'Please...' She gulped as his hard thighs brushed against hers beneath the water; his hand slid lower, curving around her waist, then eased upwards to cup the underside of her breast.

She trembled. 'Stop that!' she gasped. 'Your mother will be here any minute.'

'So?' he mocked. 'I'm a grown man, and anyway I'm sure she'd be delighted if her plan worked.'

'Plan...?' Saffron was lost.

'Don't look so worried. This is not the time.' A steward walked past with a loaded coffee-tray. 'Too many dis-tractions, but I am going to have you, Saffron, so stop trying to avoid me, hmm?'

Saffron locked the cabin door behind her and marched straight to the bathroom, shedding her dress and underwear on the way. She turned on the shower tap and stepped under the soothing spray, silently cursing Alex Statis. Thank God the boat was docking in the port of Piraeus tomorrow morning; she couldn't stand much more.

Since the morning in the pool Alex had gone out of his way to make her life hell. At every opportunity he touched her—an arm around her shoulder, even a kiss on the cheek, and, if he caught her alone, a kiss anywhere else he could reach. She tried to stop him, but her own foolish emotions seemed to leave her paralysed in his presence. He had the uncanny ability to enthral, entice and terrify her all at the same time. The others had noticed, of course, and Sylvia had actually stopped her earlier today by the pool and told her in no uncertain terms just what she thought.

'Really, Saffron, throwing yourself at Alex won't get you anywhere. He's used to your sort, and like all men he's not going to refuse something so blatantly offered. But make no mistake—I am the one he always comes back to.'

Speechless with anger at the utter unfairness of it all— it was Alex chasing her, or more exactly teasing her, not the other way around—Saffron had walked away without answering.

But tonight! She groaned out loud, recalling the scene at dinner. Anna had been sitting next to Saffron at the table and she had quietly repeated the request she had made earlier that day for Saffy to make the job permanent.

Green eyes gentle, Saffron had tried to explain her reluctance. 'I intend to start my own salon, Anna, by the end of the year; it's always been my ambition. But I promise you can be my first customer.'

'But what about my shoulder? I need you every day,' Anna whispered so that the others couldn't hear.

'In another few weeks you will be back to normal.'

'But I like having you...'

'You won't need me...' Saffron hadn't realised her voice had risen, and she shot a startled look down the table, her green eyes caught and held by Alex's devilish brown ones.

'Need you, Saffron, darling? Maybe Mama doesn't, but you know I do,' he prompted mockingly.

Complete silence greeted his comment. Horrified, Saffron glanced around the table and seven pairs of eyes were fixed assessingly on her flushed face. The eighth pair—Alex's—were lit with laughter and something deeper she didn't recognise.

She attempted to laugh off his outrageous statement, but her dry mouth would not let her. Angry at herself and him, she shot back, 'Yes, well, you would say that, Mr Statis.' Her fingers crossed beneath the table, and praying that Anna would forgive her, she added insultingly, 'After all, if I look after your mother it saves you the bother.'

His dark brows drew together, his mouth tightened to a grim line ringed with white in his tanned face and his eyes darkened to jet, his fury at the insult implicit in her comment barely contained. Saffron thought he was about to explode, but help came from an unexpected quarter: Sylvia.

'You did not have to put it so bluntly, Saffron. We all knew what Alex meant, and it is only natural that he wants his mother cared for, and I must say you and Anna do seem to get on remarkably well.'

Normal conversation resumed almost immediately, the social niceties preserved. But Saffron felt the force of Alex's anger beating down on her all through the meal, and she didn't dare look at him.

Stepping out of the shower and briskly rubbing herself dry with a large fluffy towel, she padded barefoot back into the bedroom. She stopped suddenly, her eyes going to the door. The handle was turning, and then was violently rattled.

'Open this door, Saffron; I want to talk to you,' came Alex's unmistakable deep voice.

No way, she thought, a broad grin curving her lovely mouth. She had locked the door and left the key in. Not even the master key would do any good.

Thanking God for her foresight, she crawled naked into bed, a self-satisfied smile on her face. Stroke another one up to her...

Early the next morning, as Saffron quietly opened her cabin door prior to going to Anna's, she halted in her tracks.

Sylvia, dressed in a diaphanous black négligé, her hand curved around the handle of the door opposite, held a finger to her lips and whispered, 'Shh. Alex needs his sleep; it was almost dawn...' Her lips curled in a smile; she looked like the cat that had swallowed the canary. 'Well, you know what I mean, Saffron, dear. But, with his mother on board, propriety dictates that I return to my own cabin...'

CHAPTER FOUR

SAFFRON was stunned. She closed her eyes for a second, fighting to subdue the pain spreading in her chest. She tried to tell herself it was heartburn—perfectly natural; she had not eaten yet. But she knew she was only fooling herself. She hated to admit it, but for the first time in her life she was suffering from the green-eyed monster—jealousy.

Dazed, she made her way to Anna's cabin and walked in, horrified at her blind stupidity. She was jealous of Sylvia and Alex. How had it happened? She had told herself that Alex just liked teasing her, his attentions weren't genuine, and anyway she didn't care a hoot about him even if she did enjoy their verbal sparring. But seeing Sylvia leave his room had shocked her to the core, and she was forced to admit that somewhere deep down inside she had nursed a secret hope, ever since Mykonos, that perhaps Alex did care for her.

'Good, dear, you're early. I wanted to talk to you before we have to join the others.'

Saffron raised dazed green eyes to where Anna sat propped up in bed, a tray with a coffee-jug and cups at her side. 'Talk'; she had heard that much.

'Yes, come and sit down and have a coffee.' Like a robot Saffron did as she said, taking the proffered cup and sipping the hot brew thirstily. 'About last night, Saffron. I think I might have misled you slightly in the past weeks. Actually my son and I have a very good relationship, and I do see him a lot more than I led you to believe. But the accident made me feel down. Alex was in Australia, and I was wallowing in self-pity.'

Saffron's head shot up and she saw the guilty smile on Anna's face. 'Misled me?'

'Yes, well, ordinarily Alex is in London every month; he has his own place but he calls to see me or telephones me almost daily. Plus in the autumn we holiday together at the villa on Serendipidos. He really is a very caring son and would not shunt me off with just anyone.'

Saffron wasn't even surprised! Now she knew why Anna had not been shocked when Alex had appeared at the café in Rhodes. But, frightened by her own reaction to him, she wanted to believe the worst of him.

'I know, Anna, and the comment I made last night was more in self-defence. Your son seems to delight in teasing me, I realise now.' Especially after seeing Sylvia this morning, she thought sadly. 'He doesn't mean anything by it.'

'Oh, I'm so glad you understand, because Alex is really quite soft-hearted beneath that hard exterior of his, and I don't want you to think badly of him, especially as he seems to like you.'

Like her? What a joke! He liked anything in a skirt, Saffron thought, and it gave her no joy.

'Plus I want you to come with me to Serendipidos in the autumn. It's a beautiful place; you will really enjoy it. You convinced me last night that you don't want a permanent job, but it will only mean extending your contract by a week or two.'

Saffron's face fell. Weeks in the vicinity of Alex was not something she could look forward to with equanimity. Her body reacted in the strangest way whenever he was near, and yet there was something about him that subconsciously repelled her. She didn't understand it at all.

Anna, as if sensing her disquiet, added, 'Well, it is a long way ahead, but think about it. Sun and sea—a lot better than autumn in England.'

Saffron held up her hand. 'OK, Anna, you've convinced me.' The shock of this morning had cured her growing fascination with Alex once and for all, and by the time she had spent the summer in London with Anna she would have got over her peculiar attraction to the man, she told herself sensibly.

Breakfast was a buffet on the poop deck, a kind of casual chaos. In the middle of it a car arrived to take James and Andreas into Athens, and hasty goodbyes were exchanged. Alex coolly instructed Saffron to have everything ready for Anna and herself to depart by helicopter for the airport, where a private jet was waiting to take them directly to London. He intended to accompany the rest of the party into Athens; his head office was there, and he needed to work.

Following the steward carrying their bags to the helipad on the top of the yacht, Saffron was feeling slightly piqued. The least Alex could have done was to be around to say goodbye to his mother, she thought, not for a second admitting that she was peeved because he hadn't seen fit to say goodbye to her either.

The blades were already in motion on the big black insect-like machine as she and Anna waited while the steward loaded the luggage.

'Mama, I almost missed you. Have a good flight and I'll be in touch soon.'

Saffron turned her head at the sound of Alex's voice. He had stopped on the opposite side of Anna, his dark head bent to kiss the older woman on the cheek. Saffron's eyes widened in amazement as he straightened up and looked directly at her. Gone was the casually dressed man of the past week and in his place was a sombrely dressed businessman. He was wearing an expensively tailored navy three-piece suit, the jacket fitting snugly across his broad shoulders, the trousers elegantly tracing his long legs, a white silk shirt in stark contrast to his tanned complexion and a conservative navy and grey striped tie at his throat. A black leather briefcase in one hand completed the picture of a ruthless tycoon. Her whole body clenched in shock.

'You can leave now,' Alex drawled, but she did not hear him say that the pilot was waiting or that he would see her in London, and, like a thunderbolt, it hit her.

She did know him! Had done for seven years... She must have said something that passed as goodbye, she thought distractedly as she urged Anna towards the waiting helicopter. She did not see Alex's frowning glance or the intense scrutiny in his dark eyes as she climbed aboard. She could not get away fast enough...

She was intensely grateful for the noise in the helicopter that prevented her having to talk to Anna. She needed the time to collect her own thoughts...

Seven years ago, the first day at her first job after finishing college that also turned out to be her last day at the supposedly exclusive health club. The man standing in Reception saying, 'You can leave now,' and her own furious anger and embarrassment as for one long moment she had stared at the owner of the place. A tall, dark man in a navy suit, briefcase in hand, and contemptuous black eyes that burned into her skull. She had not said a word but had run out never to return. A bitter, cynical smile curved her soft lips; Alex Statis was that man. She would stake her life on it.

A tug on her arm by Anna, and she realised that the helicopter was circling to land at the far side of the airport. But Saffron was in no position to take in her surroundings; as if in a dream she helped Anna from the helicopter and followed the pilot across to a waiting jet some hundred yards away. Still in a state of shock she sank down into the seat beside Anna and barely spoke as the jet took off.

Luckily for Saffron, Anna slept almost the whole journey, only rousing to eat a perfectly prepared meal and then dozing off again. By the time Saffron sank down on the familiar white-lace-draped four-poster bed in Anna's London home late that night, alone at last, she felt sick to her soul.

How she had managed to hide her distraught state from Anna for the past few hours was a miracle, she thought with a grim smile. In fact she was not sure that she had, because over dinner Anna had asked her if anything was wrong. She had quickly reassured her that she was fine, just a bit jet-lagged, but had felt an absolute fraud when Anna had insisted that she go to bed and forget about her massage for tonight.

Private yacht, private airplane, this lovely house, dotted with antiques, a whole island for heaven's sake! She ground her teeth in sheer rage. Some would say she was lucky to be living in such an environment. Except that Saffron knew where some of the money had come from, and a few questions to Anna had convinced her that the older woman didn't.

Over dinner Saffron had deliberately turned the conversation to Alex's business, and finally asked the question that had plagued her all day.

'Does he own health clubs in London? I seem to remember hearing of one in Wimbledon,' she'd said, and had mentioned the name.

Anna's response had confirmed what Saffron already knew. 'I vaguely remember hearing the name somewhere but I really have no idea, Saffy. When Alex took over the family shipping business it was in a sorry state; he had to work like a slave to make it profitable. He has expanded into all sorts of things over the years. I can't keep up with him; I'm hopeless at business—much prefer the arts. But Alex is quite famous in his own way. The gossip columns seem to enjoy reporting his numerous affairs, unfortunately.'

Now, sitting on the bed, Saffron let her head drop into her hands. She thought about Eve, her one true friend who had died so pitifully young; it was Alex Statis and men like him who had driven her to it. She rubbed the moisture from her eyes and, stripping off her clothes, took a quick shower in the adjoining *en suite* and then crawled into bed, her mind in turmoil.

Who said crime doesn't pay? she thought scathingly. It had certainly paid for Alex. Anna had told her earlier, when waffling on about their coming trip in the autumn, that only a few years ago Alex had completely demolished the villa on Serendipidos and replaced it with a much grander one... On the proceeds of his ill-gotten gains, Saffron thought, hatred and loathing for the man swamping her tired mind. She closed her eyes and prayed for sleep but it would not come. Instead she was eighteen again...

Saffron glanced once more at her gold wristwatch—eight-thirty—then back again to the entrance door of the small pub in Covent Garden. Eve was already half an hour late; she resolved to give her five more minutes then leave. It was sad but true; the two girls were drifting apart. It had to happen, she thought sadly. Eve had left the orphanage long before she had, and gone to live in an apartment with another girl, somewhere in the East End. Whereas Saffron, on leaving the orphanage, had taken up residence at thc YWCA.

She had finished college in June a qualified beauty therapist and aromatherapist, and for the past two months had been looking for a job in a health club, salon, anything, but so far without much luck. When her parents had died so tragically young, the house had been sold, but after the debts and expenses had been paid there had not been much left to be put in trust for Saffron. On her eighteenth birthday she had inherited almost two thousand pounds and her mother's gold watch. But her nest-egg was quickly diminishing while she looked for work. Her only social life was a once-a-month meeting with Eve.

'Saffron, darling, sorry I'm late but we couldn't find a parking place.'

Saffron lifted her head and smiled. Eve was a tall, well-endowed blonde, and tonight she looked flushed and happy.

'Sorry I can't stop but Rick, my new boyfriend, is parked on double yellow lines. He's gorgeous, Saffron, and, better yet, rich. I only called in to give you this card. It's the address of an exclusive health club in Wimbledon, Studio 96—Rick has a share in it. Go to-morrow at eleven, mention Rick's name and the job of masseur is yours.' Eve blew a kiss, called, 'Ciao!' and left.

If only it had been that simple, Saffron thought as she tossed restlessly on the bed. With hindsight she realised she had been terribly naïve, but at the time it had seemed like a gift from the gods.

She had attended the interview the next day with a rather hard-faced women who was the manageress. As soon as she had mentioned Rick and produced the card she had been given the job, and told to start the next day at twelve. Saffron had had no qualms; the building was in an excellent area and was elegantly furnished, and a conducted tour had shown her a gym and spa, sauna, and the various individual cubicles for massage. The manageress had even warned her that any employer found offering sexual intercourse to the patrons would be immediately dismissed. It was a club favoured by leading members of society, from aristocrats to Members of Parliament, and they came expecting to relieve their tension and relax—nothing more!

The following day she was shown to a cubicle and told that her first client would be arriving at twelve-fifteen for a full massage. Slipping on her overall and with her personal belongings stowed in a small locker, she greeted her first client, a rather overweight middle-aged gentleman.

Slightly nervous, she instructed the gentleman to remove his robe, wrap a towel around his waist and lie face down on the bed while she went to collect the required oils. On her return the man was lying down, and she began the massage as she had been taught by her tutor. In most reputable establishments when massaging a man one only did the back, the arms and shoulders, and the feet and legs as far as the knee. Anything more and male masseurs were usually employed.

Fifteen minutes later all hell broke loose, when the man turned over and said brutally, 'Hurry up, girl. You know the muscle I want relaxing and it sure as hell isn't my back.'

To Saffron's absolute horror he grabbed her small hand and forced it towards a very personal part of him. She did the only thing she could think of: picking up the dish containing the remainder of the oil, her eyes closed, she hit him with it.

He gave a howl of outrage. 'What the hell do you think you're playing at? I paid good money and I'm not being fobbed off with a bloody back-rub.'

Saffron flung the robe over him, grabbed her coat and bag from the locker and shot straight out of the cubicle, heading for the exit, her face flaming.

'What on earth . . . ?' the manageress exclaimed. She was standing at the desk, a tall, dark-suited businessman standing beside her, a briefcase in his hand. 'Where do you think you're going, girl? You have a client.'

'I thought this was supposed to be the *crème de la crème*.' The fat man, a robe pulled over his nakedness, had followed her. 'Your prices certainly are.' He was all bluster and Saffron could only stare at him, numb with horror and disgust. Then the tall businessman turned around and she saw his face. It was Alex Statis...

'Maybe I can help you, sir.'

'You the owner? Well, for the money I paid, I expect expert service, not some bloody little amateur who hasn't a clue.'

'Why, you...!' Saffron's short, platinum-blonde hair, like a silver cap on her small head, did not prevent her true red-headed temper from flaring out of control even though she was terrified. 'You fat blubber of lard, you're a disgrace...'

She got no further as the tall stranger caught her arm and ushered her towards the door.

'You can leave now.'

She never heard what else he said. Her terrified green eyes clashed with contemptuous black for a long moment, before she took to her heels and ran.

Three days later Eve appeared at the YWCA to ask how the job was going. Saffron told her the place was no health club, but a very up-market massage parlour only one step removed from a brothel as far as she could see. A grey area in law maybe, but very lucrative for the owners. They finally ended up roaring with laughter about it, Eve declaring that her years in the orphanage and then working for a living in a supermarket must have blunted her instincts, and they both knew what she meant.

Eve had been taken into care because her parents were drug addicts, and had killed themselves with an overdose. The social services had moved in and put Eve in the orphanage. Saffron could only imagine the horrid childhood of her friend, but her loyalty to Eve was one hundred per cent, had been ever since the day she had saved her from the boy groping her.

Saffron stirred uncomfortably on the wide bed as the black bile of sheer hatred rose in her throat, threatening to choke her. She hauled herself up into a sitting position, her small hands clenched in fists, as she fought down her rage. If the incident had ended that day at the YWCA, Saffron might have been able to forget the part Alex Statis had played. But it had not... To think that she had allowed Alex to kiss her, touch her; it made her flesh creep. Alex Statis deserved to pay for the lives he had helped destroy as part-owner of that sordid club.

She remembered Eve as a teenager, large and laughing, loyal and protective of her friend. Over the next year Saffron had worked in a small beauty clinic and had seen less of Eve as the other girl's relationship with Rick continued. Then Saffron had got a live-in job at a health spa in Scotland and had left London. They'd kept in touch by letter until the day Saffron's latest letter was returned address unknown.

Saffron had stayed three years in the Highlands before returning to London and starting work at the home beauty agency. She'd shared a flat with two others, and spent her spare time improving her craft. Doing voluntary work in a local hospital, she'd developed a special interest in clinical beauty therapy. She'd loved showing women, who for various reasons, from birthmarks to those who needed to use a prosthesis as result of face cancer, how to use make-up to cover their disabilities.

Then ten months ago a policeman had arrived at Saffron's door with the information that Eve was dead. She had left a letter for Saffron, and the police had traced her through her income tax returns. In the letter Eve had explained how she had, at Rick's insistence, ended up working in the massage parlour Saffron had run out of, fulfilling the demeaning task of massaging fully the male clients, who then went smugly home to their wives in the belief that they had not technically been unfaithful... Eve had hated the job and had started to drink and take drugs to get her through the day. Rick had dumped her, and she'd felt she had nothing left to live for.

But the final paragraph had been an exhortation to Saffron to succeed.

> You have it all, Saffron—the looks, the character and the expertise to make it on your own. Not like me. I was born a loser. Promise me, Saffron, you won't let some bastard of a man get at you. Stick to your dream. Start your own business, be your own boss. Do it for me. You show them.

Saffron had been devastated. She had attended the inquest the following day, and the only slight relief had been that the coroner had returned an open verdict, not prepared to say that Eve had deliberately overdosed on drugs and alcohol. Saffron had arranged the funeral and she had been the only one at the ceremony.

She groaned out loud and slid down into the bed. Here she was, living in the house, eating the food, taking the pay of the diabolical fiend who owned the club... What was she going to do? She could not blame Anna; it had nothing to do with her; of that Saffron was sure. But she hoped and prayed that she would never have to set eyes on Alex Statis again as long as she lived.

Anna would be hurt, but Saffron had no choice. Much as she liked Anna she would have to leave, and with that thought worrying her mind she tossed restlessly all night and when, finally, dawn broke the sky, she still had not found the comforting oblivion of sleep. But not for a second dared she admit that the thought of never seeing Alex again hurt even more than the knowledge of the despicable lengths he would go to make money.

A few hours later, heavy-eyed, she completed Anna's massage, and mentioned leaving. 'I know my contract is for six months, Anna, and I've only completed a little over one, but I...'

'What is it really, Saffy? Something is bothering you; You've been quiet ever since we left the boat. Is it me? Am I too much trouble for you?'

Saffron felt an absolute heel. How did one tell a woman that her son was the lowest of the low, and you couldn't bear the thought of ever having to see him again?

'I could increase your salary.'

'No, no, you're more than generous. It was just I— Oh, nothing! Anna, forget I mentioned it.' She couldn't hurt her, and if that meant having to stay here and run the risk of seeing Alex again then so be it. She would just have to bite the bullet and disguise her hatred of the man.

The only trouble was, she thought grimly a few hours later, she had not expected to have to do it so soon! Anna had been lying down in her room, resting, and Saffron had taken the opportunity to do some hand-washing at the sink in the utility-room, when the telephone had rung. She'd known that Mrs Chambers had gone shopping, so, quickly drying her hands, she'd nipped into the kitchen and picked up the wall-mounted telephone.

'Mrs Statis's residence,' she intoned breathlessly.

'Saffron. I was hoping you would answer.' Even over the telephone there was no mistaking Alex's deep drawl. 'Are you missing me, green eyes?'

Her first thought was to slam down the receiver but she stopped herself just in time. Fighting down the rage that just the sound of his voice invoked, she replied coldly, 'I'm afraid your mother is sleeping at the moment, Mr Statis; perhaps you could call back later.'

'I did not ask for Mama, I asked if you missed me,' Alex corrected her in a teasing tone. 'Why the frozen air, Saffron, sweet? Sulking because I'm not there with you?'

'No. Thanking God you're miles away! Goodbye.' And she slammed down the receiver, her hand trembling with the force of her anger. The man's conceit was only surpassed by his enormous ego. Bitter hatred consumed her. If there was any way on God's earth she could make him pay for what he had done, she would. The telephone rang again. She was torn between letting it ring and possibly waking Anna, or answering it and hearing the hateful voice again.

Duty won. 'Yes?' she snapped.

'No one puts the telephone down on me. Do I make myself clear Saffron?' His former easy amusement had vanished; he was now back to being a hard-voiced autocrat.

'Mr Statis, I have told you, your mother is sleeping. I have no wish to speak to you, not now, not ever. Do I make myself clear?' she drawled with icy cynicism.

'Something has happened; you sound different.'

She was different; she was no longer the naïve innocent, helplessly surrendering to his practised seductive charm. Just the sound of his voice, which she had once thought deep and rich, now filled her with loathing.

'Saffron! Are you still there?'

'Yes, sir.'

'Cut out the sarcasm and tell me what has happened. Did you discover Mama is a fake? Is that it?'

'I see no point in this conversation, and unless you have a message for your mother I really must go.' The only fake Saffron had discovered was Alex Statis and the rage was like a festering sore inside her.

'Yes, OK, I'll be in touch.'

Not if I can help it, she thought grimly, replacing the receiver.

Saffron strategically placed the lounger in the back garden of the house to catch the sun's rays and settled down to soak up the sun. She had driven Anna to her Friday afternoon bridge game and the next few hours were her own. Who needs foreign holidays, she mused, when late June in England is just about perfect? Warm days and long light nights.

By a bit of judicious questioning she had established from Anna that Alex was not expected any time in the near future, and she remembered her telling her that when he did come to London he had his own apartment, so her fear of seeing the man had abated over the past two weeks. She knew he telephoned every day but she had found it relatively easy to vanish when he called.

Anna had improved in leaps and bounds and her shoulder was completely better. In fact Saffron felt that she was taking her salary on false pretences but Anna would not hear of her leaving. Plus there was the small problem of having nowhere to stay. She didn't want to waste any of her savings on an apartment when very shortly she would have her own property.

To Saffron's surprise, she had discovered that Anna was a much livelier lady than she had first thought. Together they had attended various art exhibitions, the theatre, an outdoor opera. The woman was a committed culture buff. At last night's poetry reading in Anna's elegant sitting-room Saffron had hardly been able to contain her amusement as the latest 'darling boy' waffled on about 'Chopsticks', the symbolism escaping Saffron completely.

A smile on her lips at the memory, she closed her eyes and gently dozed.

'Perfect Sleeping Beauty waiting for her prince.'

Saffron's eyes snapped open and she was horrified to find Alex Statis standing staring down at her. She hauled herself up to a sitting position, stiff with outrage at his unheralded arrival. 'And instead she gets the toad,' she drawled, her head high, her eyes blazing hatred.

One dark brow arched enquiringly at the biting sarcasm in her tone. 'I had hoped for a more enthusiastic welcome after deserting my office simply to come and look after you and Mama.'

'You shouldn't have bothered. Your mother and I can manage perfectly well on our own.' She glanced up; over his tall frame he was still wearing a business suit, and the last lingering doubt vanished from her mind. It was the same man.

'I'm sure you can, Saffron,' he agreed as he shrugged off his jacket and dropped it on the ground. With one hand he deftly loosened the tie at his throat and flicked open the top three buttons of his shirt, his dark eyes openly laughing at her. 'But who am I to spoil my mama's enjoyment? She has refused to allow me to speak to you on the telephone, so I have, as a dutiful son, decided to play her game and spend the next few weeks here.'

So that was why it had been so easy to avoid his calls. Anna had made sure of it, and Saffron could not help wondering why even as she responded icily, 'Your mother and I can enjoy ourselves without you.' If he was staying she was leaving!

She watched as he lowered his long frame on to the soft green grass beside her chair, long legs stretched out before him in lazy ease, his hands clasped behind his head, his face lifted to the sun.

'Hardly the welcome I was hoping for. Alone at last!' he drawled mockingly. 'Isn't this where you tell me you missed me?'

'Missed you!' she exclaimed parrot fashion. 'Like a hole in the head.' The man must be mad.

'I can see my dear mama has not revealed her little game yet.' His eyes were closed, thick dark lashes curving on his bronzed skin; he looked vulnerable but Saffron knew better.

'What game?' she demanded coldly.

'You, my dear Saffron, are one in a long line of sup- posedly *good* women my mother parades before me every summer under the guise of a companion, whatever, in a vain attempt to get me married off.' He looked up at her, a cynical smile slashing his hard face. 'You should be flattered; you have done better than most; usually I have them out of my life in days.'

Saffron slid her hands under her thighs, fighting down the urge to claw his eyes out. The conceited jerk! He moved to lie on his side, one elbow on the ground, his hand propping his head, so that he could watch her easily, his long body at ease. Even as she hated him she recognised that he was devilishly attractive, all virile male, but superimposed on his face she saw the image of Eve's coffin. She blinked, blotting out the picture.

'My dear mama could put Machiavelli to shame; surely you have realised that by now, Saffron?' he opined lightly, shooting her a questioning glance.

Despite herself Saffron was intrigued as Alex con- tinued. 'Mind you, I have to admit she has surpassed herself this time. I got the report on you yesterday in Athens, and you check out perfectly. There's no doubt that Mama's cover stories are certainly improving,' he drawled with fond amusement.

Saffron was so furious that she did not trust herself to speak. He actually thought her job with Anna was simply a ploy to spike his interest. He had the nerve to have her investigated, when he operated on the very edge of the law himself. What an ego the swine had...

'Last year Mother hired a Greek teacher who couldn't speak more than three sentences, the year before a librarian to catalogue her books, all fifty of them,' he reminisced, a wide smile softening his harsh features, his deep brown eyes laughing up at her, inviting her to share the joke. 'You are her latest marriage bait, and if I were the marrying kind I might just be tempted,' he suggested with a cynical sensuality that made her shudder.

Saffron turned her head away and looked around the garden, anywhere but at the man lying at her feet. She remembered how she had almost succumbed to Alex's easy charm, his kiss, his caress. God! What might have happened if she had not finally recognised him? The very idea made her sick to the stomach. She drew in a painful breath and got to her feet, giving Alex's sprawled body a contemptuous glance. 'You flatter yourself, Mr Statis. I would not marry you if you were the last man on earth,' she said thickly. 'Excuse me.'

In one lithe movement Alex was at her side, his hand on her naked shoulder.

'Don't touch me!' she cried, knocking his hand away.

Alex's nostrils flared as he sucked in an angry breath. 'I wasn't aware my touch was so abhorrent to you.'

'Well, you are now.'

His eyes narrowed assessingly on her pale face. 'There is something different about you.'

Yes, you evil swine; I know how you make money. She didn't say it but the contempt in her icy green eyes said it for her. 'If Anna confirms what you have just told me I'm leaving. I refuse to provide entertainment for your sort.'

'My sort?' A hint of steel entered his voice. 'Why do I get the impression you have just insulted me?'

'Probably because I did.' She was in no mood to bandy words with a man little better than a pimp. 'Get out of my way; I'm leaving.' Alex was standing barely a foot away, blocking her path back to the house.

'No. You can't leave. I will not have Mama upset. She likes you, and you signed a six-month contract, and I intend to make sure you fulfil it, or I will sue you for every penny you have, or ever will have.'

Saffron's head tilted back; her green eyes, flashing fire, clashed with the black implacability of Alex's, and she knew he meant every word. All trace of amusement gone, he was once more the harsh-faced stranger of her memory. 'Yes, I just bet you would,' she sneered, not bothering to hide her contempt.

His look was every bit as contemptuous as hers. 'You disappoint me, Saffron; challenging a man to gain his interest is the oldest trick in the book. I almost believed you were innocent of any involvement in Mama's plan. I thought you were above such games.' He lifted his hand and caught hold of her chin. Her hands balled into fists at her sides, but she refused to struggle, even though her heart began to pound as he gave her a scorching look. 'But if that's the way you want to play it I'll oblige.'

'I have no desire to play, and certainly not with you,' she said flatly.

'But I do, Saffron; you intrigue me.' His voice dropped to a husky growl 'Along with a host of other feelings I fully intend to explore.'

Before she had a chance to do more than register that he was about to kiss her, his head lowered and his lips claimed hers. Saffron instantly froze. Shocked by the harsh possession of his mouth, she shuddered as his arms enfolded her, and his hand slid to her buttocks, pressing her into his hard thighs. Stunned by the speed of his assault, she almost responded to the fevered urgency of his caress. His hand stroked down her naked thigh, binding her tightly to the hard heat of his body.

It was his guttural, 'I want you,' and the realisation of his aroused state that stopped her. How many women had he said the exact same words to? How many had succumbed to his persuasive charm? As Eve had with Rick, his partner, only to end up working in a massage parlour. The sickening knowledge of how he had made his money turned the blood to ice in her veins.

Sensing her lack of response, Alex lifted his head; his dark eyes, black with frustrated desire, searched her pale face. He sucked in a deep, steadying breath and gently put her away from him. His gaze lingered over her scantily clad form and then he glanced down at his suit.

'You're right, I'm hardly dressed for the part and anyone might interrupt us. When I make love to you for the first time, I want you on your own with no fear of interruptions.' He turned, adding, 'I'll see you later,' with a certainty that incensed Saffron into losing her temper completely.

'Not if I see you first,' she screeched after him, derision twisting her delicate features. A cheeky wave of his hand indicated that he had heard her, and was not the least fazed by her angry outburst.

CHAPTER FIVE

SAFFRON watched his departure, his lithe walk, the proud set of his head and shoulders. Her eyes drifted briefly around the garden, and she thought of his wealth and eminent respectability, then her glance rested once more on his broad back as he entered the house, and she longed to put a knife in it...

No. He wasn't worth going to prison for. But with the hot sun incapable of warming the ice in her veins Saffron silently vowed that if there was any way to make Alex Statis's life hell she would do it. She owed it to Eve. It was the Alexes of this world who, in the avid pursuit of money, flirted with the law and exploited and demeaned women.

Saffron's eyes glittered, her small hands clenched into fists. She would have her revenge on Mr Statis supposing it took her a lifetime to find a way...

But she found a way a lot quicker than she could have hoped...

'I owe you an apology, Saffron.' Alex's dark eyes gleamed golden in the flickering light of the candle in the centre of the table. They were dining in a small, intimate French restaurant, at Alex's insistence.

Earlier, Saffron had picked Anna up from her bridge party and Alex had been waiting when they returned. Saffron had tactfully withdrawn to her room and left mother and son alone. It had been a mistake! On returning to the living-room an hour later Alex was still in evidence, and in a few moments had hustled Saffron

81

into having dinner with him. Anna had been no support at all as Saffron had tried to turn down the invitation. She was forced to the conclusion that Alex was probably right about his mother's machiavellian tendencies.

'An apology—from you?'

'Surprising, I know, but I had a word with Mama this evening. She told me all about her accident; it was silly of her to keep it from me in the first place. I have no intention of having her live with me; it would be much too confining. I have set her mind at rest on that score and she assures me you are innocent of any plan to trap me.'

Bully for him, the condescending swine; was she supposed to be flattered that he was absolving her from any conspiracy? she thought, eyeing him almost clinically. He was wearing a conventional black dinner-suit, white silk shirt and dark bow-tie. He wore his clothes with an elegance that few men possessed, and she knew that beneath the outer garments his body was a perfect example of the masculine form; he could put Michelangelo's David to shame. A few weeks ago she would have been intimidated by such raw masculine perfection, but not now. The inside was rotten to the core.

She glanced at his face. He was smiling complacently.

'So how about we start again from scratch——' his hand reached out and covered hers where it lay on the table '—and develop this chemistry, or whatever it is between us, to its logical conclusion?'

'Why not?' she murmured, the germ of an idea so preposterous that she wondered at her own daring taking root in her head, and, deliberately squeezing his hand, she added a husky, 'Yes.'

His brown eyes flashed with pure masculine triumph. 'Good; let's skip dessert and go to my apartment.' Alex spoke throatily, virtually dragging her to her feet. He flung a bundle of notes on the table and without letting go of her hand steered her out of the restaurant and into his waiting black Jaguar.

Saffron was seething at his arrogant, high-handed treatment, but she forced herself not to let it show. Alex started the car with a crash of gears. He was inpatient, and desire or lust—it did not matter which—made his usual steady hand shake, she noted cynically. Battling down her hatred for the man, she gritted her teeth and deliberately moved closer to rest her head on his broad shoulder, allowing her hand to fall teasingly on to his hard thigh.

Alex hardly spoke as he urged her out of the car in the underground car park, and into the lift. As the doors slid closed he hauled her into his arms. She closed her eyes and fought down her disgust at being held fast against the hard muscles of his body. Her lips parted at the thrusting force of his tongue invading her mouth, and she forced herself not to shove him away as she longed to do, her stomach curling in revulsion. But was it? she wondered, her legs weakening as his hands travelled the length of her body with a hard sureness that made her tremble.

Luckily the lift stopped and the doors slid open. 'Alex,' she said softly, pushing against the hard wall of his chest. 'We've arrived.'

'Thank God!' he groaned, lifting his head and looking down at her with black, passion-filled eyes.

There was only one door in the wide corridor, and Alex slipped the key into the lock with a hand that shook slightly. Then, turning, with a hand in the small of her back, he ushered her inside the apartment.

Saffron looked around with interest, and was surprised to note that the place had a homely air, not at all what she had expected. Pictures of his relatives and friends vied with what were obviously paintings by the masters. What looked like a Monet had pride of place over a large pine-framed fireplace. Big deep buttoned hide chairs and a couple of sofas were strategically placed to get the benefit of the fire and view. The curtains were open and the whole of London seemed to be reflected in the plate-glass windows.

'I can't believe you're here, Saffron.' Alex's deep voice interrupted her musing, and once more she was caught in his arms. 'You have no idea how much I want you. From the moment you felled me in Rhodes, I've ached to get you in my bed.' His lips showered tiny kisses on her eyes her cheek, the tip of her nose, all over her face, and Saffron was shocked by the gentleness in his gaze.

'I told myself it was because I wanted to punish you.' His lips moved caressingly down the slender arch of her throat as she tipped her head back, trying to escape his marauding mouth. But it didn't work; her pulse-rate soared and she was in danger of forgetting why she was here.

'Punish me?' she murmured. It was Alex who needed punishing and she had to remember that.

'I know; stupid macho pride. But after Mykonos I realised I wanted you any way I could have you. I didn't even care if you were part of Mama's scheme. Seeing you in this dress again tonight reminded me.' She was wearing her Ralph Lauren, the only formal dress she possessed, and he put his hand on her covered shoulder. 'That night on the *Lion Lore* I nearly lost it when you walked into the dining-room, you looked so beautiful, but I couldn't do anything about it with all the guests around.'

He was good—very good! Saffron recognised. The sensual spell he was weaving with tender words and caresses was almost believable. But then he'd had plenty of practice, she thought grimly, the mood broken by his glib lie. Guests had not stopped him sharing his bed with

Sylvia. She leant sharply back from him, but he did not release her.

'I tried to stay away but the last two weeks without seeing you were hell. I found myself missing your red hair and flashing eyes. I thought of you at the most inopportune times, until today I realised I had to do something about it.'

His mouth nuzzled her neck and his hands found the zip at side of her dress. She was perilously close to forgetting why she was here, and, gathering every ounce of self-control she possessed, she pushed him harder.

'Wait, Alex.' She deliberately lowered her voice, a slight tremor to her tone that wasn't all play-acting, unfortunately. 'You said to follow this chemistry to its logical conclusion. But marriage is a big step—are you sure you're ready for it? You have been a bachelor an awfully long time.'

'Marriage? Who the bloody hell mentioned marriage?' He let go of her and stepped back as if he had been stung, and she had to bite her lip to force back the laughter that bubbled up inside her at the expression of shock and horror on his rugged face.

'I'm sorry if I misunderstood,' she said softly, acting for all she was worth. 'But I'm afraid that's the only way you'll ever get me.'

Alex's dark eyes narrowed dangerously. 'If I thought you really meant that I could prove you wrong in five minutes,' he declared hardly. He reached out and ran one long finger delicately from her jaw to her throat over her one naked shoulder and on to the tip of her breast, lightly covered by the soft fabric of her dress. She forced herself to show no response, but her breast hardened to a taut peak beneath his cool manipulation. His dark look turned to one of indolent satisfaction at her body's reaction. 'Make that two minutes,' he amended mockingly.

'God, what an ego!' she jeered, and, deliberately turning her back on him, she headed for the door.

Alex moved swiftly; hard hands caught hold of her arms and spun her around to face him. 'Nobody turns their back on me, lady.'

'Let me go.'

His dark eyes became cold and assessing on her flushed face. 'Why fight it? You want me. Surely you're not going to pretend you're shy?' he said cynically. 'Massage is a pretty personal profession. Hundreds of men must have felt the gentle caress of your hands, Saffron, and ached for more. Did you demand marriage from all of them before granting their wish? I think not...'

One dark brow arched sardonically. 'Playing the innocent does not fool me for one second. No woman gets to your age without knowing the game. So don't try and make the stakes too high, or I might just decide the game isn't worth the candle.'

Saffron despised him at that moment more than she had thought possible. She had worked hard for her career and did not need this immoral, greedy pig sneering at her. She began to struggle, her small hands trying to prise his from her arms, hating the lazy strength with which he held her, but it was no use...

'You have an overrated belief in your charms, Mr Statis,' she spat. He honestly thought she would fall into his arms like a ripe plum; well, he was in for a very rude awakening. 'Let go of me.'

'You're hardly going to convince me to marry you with the hands-off technique.' His smile was without humour. 'I never buy without sampling first.'

'That I can believe,' she snorted disgustedly; knowing how low he would stoop to make money, she wouldn't put anything past him.

'So why the outrage?'

His gaze slid down the length of her body, lingering on her breast and thigh; she had to force herself not to flinch under his intense scrutiny, and when his eyes fixed on her flushed and furious face once more, her green eyes spitting hatred, his brows drew together in a thoughtful frown.

'You've changed since the yacht. On board you were flustered, embarrassed by my attentions maybe, but always receptive. Now——'

'Now we are virtually alone, and you're much more dangerous...' Saffron cut in. If she was going to go through with her plan for revenge, she was going to have to be a lot more careful. She couldn't let Alex suspect for an instant just how much she despised him.

He gave her a long, speculative look. 'So you're saying you're frightened of me, or is it of yourself?'

'Maybe a bit of both,' she said lightly. 'You're a fast worker, A—Alex.' She almost choked on his hateful name, but to her amazement he mistook her stammer for feminine emotion.

'Saffron, you sweet fool, I would never hurt you — quite the reverse. I only want to make love to you.' The last came out on a triumphant groan as his arms moved around her, moulding her body to his while his lips covered hers.

Every instinct she possessed begged her to break free from the demand of his mouth moving over hers, his hard body pressed so close that she could feel the rapid pounding of his heart, the strength of his arms as he lifted and carried her across the room to deposit her gently on the sofa, his great size lowering over her. But she closed her eyes and fought the desire to shove him away and run screaming from the apartment.

No. She would suffer his kisses and caresses to a point and no further, and eventually, when he was desperate to possess her, she would reiterate her demand for marriage. If she had read his character right he was a man who never accepted defeat, and when she finally had his ring on her finger she would tell him the truth, and take him for every penny she could get. She didn't want it for herself, but there were plenty of charities in the world, and far too many orphanages, and if anyone deserved to pay it was Alex Statis.

'Saffron, where did you go?' She opened her eyes. Alex was staring down at her, a chagrined look on his harsh features. 'I must be losing my touch,' he said with a husky chuckle.

Saffron didn't believe him for one moment: his male ego was too huge for him to imagine that a woman might not find him irresistible. But not by a flicker of an eyelash did she betray her thoughts. Instead she wound her slender arms around his neck and lifted her head for his mouth. 'You caught me by surprise, knocked the breath from my body,' she offered, her slender fingers tangling through the dark hair at the back of his neck, when what she really wanted to do was strangle the devil . . .

She'd thought that it would be easy to suffer his kiss, but realised he was far too astute; she had to make some response, and, opening her mouth over his, she flicked her tongue against his lips. She felt his large body jerk at her tentative caress, and was congratulating herself on her acting ability when insidiously the kiss changed. She was no longer the instigator; Alex had taken over.

The slow kiss became a blazing statement of intent. His tongue plunged in the deep, moist interior of her mouth as his hand smoothed down between their two bodies. She trembled as heat suddenly ignited in her stomach, and his mouth moved down over her firm breast and began to suckle it through the fabric of her dress. She arched and gasped at the same time, mortified by the force of her reaction.

No! her mind screamed. This could not be happening; his touch revolted her. Unfortunately, however, her body seemed incapable of absorbing the message.

Suddenly Alex's hand was on her thigh, her dress pushed up around her waist and then he was touching her intimately, urging her legs apart, his long fingers sliding beneath the edge of her briefs and stroking her soft feminine folds with devastating effect. Her eyes closed; she could not fight the incredible tide of pleasure that his touch evoked. His teeth found the top of her dress where it left one shoulder bare and pulled it roughly down, exposing her firm, full breast to his hungry eyes.

'Alex, you can't.' She knew she had to stop him, but no man had ever touched her so intimately before, and she wanted to drown in the pleasure she was experiencing.

His hand moved to stroke across her thigh, and slowly up over her hips, leaving her aching. His black eyes burnt with a triumphant masculine passion. 'Let me get you out of this and I'll show you I can,' he said arrogantly, holding her shocked eyes with his own as he stood and stripped speedily down to his briefs, then, finding the zip of her dress, eased it down her body in one swift movement.

Defensively she crossed her arms over her naked breasts. How had he got so far so fast? She didn't know, and fought to sit up, but Alex was too quick for her. He caught her hands and spread them out from her sides while he lowered his hard, near-naked body back over her.

'You're beautiful, more beautiful than I remembered,' Alex husked, glancing down at her bare breasts.

'Stop,' she demanded harshly. This had gone far enough.

'No. I want to look at you,' he said, his dark gaze, hard and hot, flashing to her face and colliding with her glittering green eyes. He moved slightly and she felt him swell against her. She looked down between their two bodies, a soft gasp escaping her, then her frantic gaze swept back to his face. His jaw tautened and she felt his body surge even more against the cradle of her womanhood. She trembled, her whole body flushing scarlet.

His hands lifted and covered the soft, creamy mounds of her breasts. 'So soft, so perfect.' He rolled his palms over the rosy peaks, bringing them to aching tips of taut arousal, and then gently he trailed his fingers around each dark aureole. 'You are so beautiful; your skin is like sun-brushed magnolia.' He took each burgeoning nipple between a finger and thumb and plucked gently, teasingly.

A line of fire shot from Saffron's breast to her groin and her body arched helplessly beneath his teasing caress. Then he leant forward, his hands curving her shoulders, and brought her up towards him, her hair flowing down her back in a riot of shimmering curls. Mindless, she lifted her face for his kiss. His night-black eyes held hers as, instead of kissing her, as she had expected, he slowly, delicately brushed his hair-roughened chest over the hard tips of her breasts and smiled a devilish, sensuous smile at her shuddering reaction.

Dear heaven! she groaned inwardly as her body instinctively curved against his chest, her lips parted softly, invitingly. She had to get away. Stop him. But his hand tracing her spine and the soft trail of his lips down her throat and around to her ear, his tongue licking around the soft whorls, sent shimmering arrows of delight through every nerve in her body.

'You and I don't need anything so antiquated as marriage, little one, or the romantic lies of undying love. Your body needs mine now.' He eased back. 'Look at your breasts, full and aching.' She glanced down as he rasped, 'The same as I am full and aching.' He hugged her to him. 'Here? Or the bedroom?' he whispered throatily against her ear. 'I'm easy, but I can't wait much longer.' His body surged against hers once more.

He was easy! he had said. God, what did that make her? Saffron thought in horror, struggling to regain her senses. She hated him and yet she had responded like a sex-starved fool.

She shoved him hard in the chest, not caring what he thought, too horrified by her turbulent emotions to hide the disgust she felt. Catching him off guard, he fell back, lost his balance and ended up on the floor.

Saffron might have found the stunned look on his face amusing at any other time, but right now she was too frustrated and furious. She scrambled to her feet, hauling her dress back on, and snarled, 'You might be easy but I'm not, Mr Statis. Hell will freeze over before I share your bed.' And, with a last contemptuous glance at his sprawled body, she took off at a run for the door.

'What the hell...? Wait, Saffron!'

He must be out of his tiny mind if he thought she was going to wait for him, Saffron thought, ignoring his shout, but suddenly she was grabbed from behind and swung round. Without giving her time to catch her breath, a bristling, angry, near-naked Alex was dragging her back to the sofa and flinging her down.

'Don't you manhandle me,' she cried, green eyes leaping with rage.

'Manhandle? I could bloody murder you, you little tease! What was that exhibition all about?' Alex demanded harshly, his eyes narrowed on her red face.

'I——' She almost told him how she really felt. Wild, irrational anger at Alex and, if she was honest, at herself almost made her tell the truth. How much she hated him... But she stopped herself just in time. Alex was clever. If she told him she would be out of a job, minus her salary, with any hope of getting revenge on the swine out of the window for good. Thinking fast, she said the one thing she thought might just work. 'I've never...' She lowered her lashes over her glittering green eyes, hoping she looked demure. 'I'm still a virgin.'

'You're what?'

'You heard,' she murmured, still not looking at him. She sensed him move towards where she sat, and felt the depression of the sofa as he sat down beside her.

'That's unbelievable; you're twenty-five... How on earth has a beautiful woman like you not been caught before now?' The incredulity in his voice was unmistakable.

'I'm not caught now,' she snapped back, and could have bitten her tongue at her hasty response.

'No?' Alex prompted softly, watching her with narrowed eyes.

'No,' she said with a shake of her head, her stormy gaze meeting him.

'Then I imagined your complete capitulation just now?' Alex's mouth assumed a cynical twist. 'Give me some credit, Saffron; I'm thirty-nine years old, not a young boy, and I have great difficulty in believing in your innocence, however bashfully you proclaim your virginity.'

The steadiness of her gaze told him exactly what she thought of his cynical tone. 'That's your problem, not mine.' She got to her feet. 'Anna will be needing me; I have to go.'

'What about my needs?' he drawled, his dark eyes gleaming with amusement. 'We are here alone; why not finish what we started?'

'No way.' Her eyes brushed over his near-nude, lounging form and she despised herself because, for a moment, she was tempted.

'Oh, there is a way,' Alex said silkily as he stepped into his trousers and pulled on his shirt. Draping his jacket over one shoulder, he added, 'Your way—marriage. But I'm not such a fool.'

'Shame, but that's my only offer,' she snapped.

'Jewels, furs, a villa in Greece. You would find me a very generous lover, Saffron. Think about it. I'll give you twenty-four hours to reconsider.'

Saffron should have been delighted that she was getting to him, but instead all she felt was fear. 'You don't believe in love and marriage,' she reminded him curtly. 'I do.'

Five minutes later, sitting in the passenger seat of Alex's elegant car, his dark, brooding presence intimidating as they sped through the streets of London, she had a horrible conviction that it was an enormous mistake to try and seek revenge from a man like Alex Statis.

'Anna, I need to ask you something and I want an honest answer,' Saffron said. Her employer was lying face down on the bed, and could not see the grim expression on her face, for which Saffron was grateful. After the fiasco of her dinner date with Alex, she had lain awake for hours, going over in her head everything he had said since arriving in London, and she recalled Alex's comment about his mother always trawling for a wife for him.

'Yes, what is it?' Anna asked lethargically.

'Your son told me yesterday that you had a habit of...' There was no other way of asking except directly. 'Well, he said you turn up with a companion every summer on the flimsiest of pretexts, trying to get him married off.'

Anna chuckled. 'I may have done once or twice. Surely you can't blame me for trying? God knows I would like some grandchildren before I die, and I'm not getting any younger; neither is Alex, come to that. He is very shortly going to be past his sell-by date, as I have told him frequently.'

'So Alex was right. That is why you employed me.' The disappointment was acute; she had honestly thought of Anna as a friend.

'No.' Anna turned over. 'Not you, Saffy. I wouldn't trick you like that. I needed you. Dr Jenkins told you.' She frowned, but her blue eyes avoided contact with Saffron. 'I still need you, and if Alex has told you anything different ignore him.'

If only she could, Saffron thought grimly, and Anna's denial was not the most convincing in the world. She wouldn't put it past the wily old woman to have set her up. Saffron was proud of her abilities and a professional to her fingertips. It hurt her pride to think that she had been tricked into working with Anna.

'He's rather too large to ignore,' she muttered drily, realising that Anna was expecting some response, and, with a quick flick of the sheet over the older woman's recumbent form, she added, 'All finished. I'll just go and wash my hands and you'd better drink some water; you know the aromatic oils can give you a headache.'

Swiftly she put the bottles of oil back in their slots in her workbag and, taking the mixing bowl, headed for Anna's bathroom. Turning on the tap of the vanity basin, she picked up the soap and began lathering her hands.

She had never thought of herself as a vengeful person, but since she'd realised that Alex part-owned the massage parlour that was really responsible for Eve's tragic death the desire for revenge had become a cancer eating at her mind every minute of the day.

She had dreamt of him last night—a dark, evil figure chasing her along a wild, wind-swept moor to the rim of a huge pit. He'd been almost upon her when the vision of Eve had lifted her to the sky, and the wild, agonised scream of the man as he'd tumbled into the black hole had echoed in her mind long after she had awakened sweating and crying. She recognised the dream as some kind of wish-fulfilment. But the crying she couldn't understand.

Turning off the tap and drying her hands, she sighed dejectedly. In theory revenge was all very well, but in practice it was nowhere near as easy. Saffron wasn't a fool; she knew that Alex desired her, wanted her—he made no secret of the fact—but how to turn his want into hurt was not so easy. She could hurt him through his mother, tell Anna how he added to the family fortune, but it did not seem fair to involve her. That left her original plan of persuading him to marry her and then leaving him on the wedding night still wanting—a massive blow to his pride and, more importantly, his pocket...

She looked at her reflection in the mirror above the basin. Was she a *femme fatale*? Cool green eyes fringed with thick brown lashes looked back at her. She had been told she was beautiful but she didn't see it herself. Her eyes were slightly slanted, and her mouth a little wide and full-lipped. Then there was the mass of ginger hair. Had there ever been a carrot-topped courtesan? She doubted it...

She slipped off her overall. Underneath she was wearing a simple cream cotton jersey sundress, shoe-string straps supporting the narrow, figure-hugging tube. Her one good point was that she had a good figure—long legs, slim hips, a tiny waist and a good bust—maybe a bit too much bust.

A vivid image of Alex nuzzling her breast last night flashed in her mind, and a shiver of fear snaked down her spine. With it came the realisation that her fool-hardy plot to seduce him into marriage was just that—foolish! However Alex made his money was of no account. He was perceived by the world at large as a respectable, wealthy entrepreneur. Sophisticated, dynamic, an expert lover, he could have any woman he wanted and he knew it...

Saffron shook her head at her reflection, her carrot curls swinging loose around her shoulders, a self-derisory smile revealing gleaming white teeth, and she chuckled. How could she have been so stupid as to imagine that she could hurt Alex by tricking him into marriage and parting with a fortune? She could no more play a *femme fatale* as fly to the moon, and the only person to get hurt would be herself. Grief at the death of her friend and the shock of recognising Alex Statis had made her act completely out of character. Thank God she had come to her senses in time!

She then felt a pang of sadness. Tilting her head back, she mouthed a silent prayer. Sorry, Eve; if there is any justice in the world Statis will get his come-uppance, but I'm not the sort to do this. Forgive me. And she imagined she heard Eve's hearty laughter echoing in her head. Suddenly she felt as if a ton weight had been lifted from her shoulders, and for the first time in weeks her usual light-hearted optimism lent a glow to her eyes and a smile to her mouth.

She was a mature adult woman, a professional with a business plan to fulfil. She would complete her contract with Anna, and avoid her son like the plague, and by the end of the year she would achieve her ambition and be the proud owner of a small beauty clinic. Her sense of proportion restored, she swung on her heel and went back into the bedroom.

Saffron froze. Alex, wearing well-washed denim jeans and a blue sweatshirt, was leaning against the bedroom door.

Anna turned moisture-filled eyes on her. 'I can't believe it, Saffy, dear.'

What was Alex doing here? And what had he said to upset his mother? 'Don't upset yourself, Anna.' She crossed to her charge and put a consoling arm around her slender shoulders, shooting Alex a vitriolic glance over his mother's head.

'I'm not upset, you silly girl; these are tears of joy. I'm delighted. You and Alex—to marry...'

'Marry.' Saffron's arm fell from Anna. She turned slightly, her eyes flying open to their widest extent as Alex crossed the room in long, lithe strides even as she spoke. 'Him,' she muttered, her mouth hanging open in amazement.

'Saffron, darling, I thought over what you said and you were right.' His arms came around her and his lips lowered towards hers.

Hoist with her own petard! immediately came to mind. But she had no more time to think, as he kissed her long and deep...

CHAPTER SIX

NUMB, paralysed, frozen in shock. No single word could describe Saffron's state of mind. She looked up into Alex's bland face, her eyes searching his for some hint as to what exactly he was playing at.

'A bit more enthusiasm would be appreciated.' His dark glance pierced hers, and it took considerable will-power to hold back an angry retort.

'You said an affair and gave me twenty-four hours,' she hissed angrily.

'So I changed my mind. Mama's watching—look happy.'

'You caught me by surprise,' she managed lightly, her mind spinning with the knowledge of the chance his proposal presented her with. She eased out of his arms only to be clasped by Anna in a motherly embrace.

'I'm so happy for you both, Saffy. Now don't worry about me; get your bag and run along with Alex to choose the ring.' She kissed Saffron's cheek and stepped back, clasping her hands in front of her, as she added, 'Oh, my! Only three days to prepare a wedding. I must dash.'

Saffron followed Alex out of the door and down the stairs still reeling. She wanted to laugh at the irony. She had just decided to forget all thoughts of revenge and avoid the man like the plague, while Alex, in a complete about-face from last night and his declaration that he did not believe in marriage, had decided to do the exact opposite.

Ten minutes later they were seated in his car moving slowly through the London traffic on their way to the jeweller's, Anna's last comment echoing in Saffron's head like a death-knell.

'Why?' she finally asked baldly, all too conscious of the tension building in the interior of the car.

He did not pretend not to know what she meant. 'I never expected to marry, and I don't usually give in to sexual teasing.' He shot her an angry, accusing glance, and she knew he was remembering last night. 'In my experience so-called decent women are out for one thing from a man—a meal-ticket for life, the wealthier the better. I have a grudging respect for whores; at least they state the price up front.'

'And of course you're an expert on the subject,' Saffron snapped scathingly, disgust and hatred making her green eyes glitter angrily.

Alex flashed a sidelong glance at her flushed face, his eyes narrowing dangerously at her heated reaction. 'No, I have never paid for a woman in my life. I have never needed to.'

Her hair-triggered temper threatened to boil over. Of course he did not pay women; instead he let them make money for him. In that second Saffron decided that revenge would be hers...

'But as for my change of heart about marriage, it is really quite simple. I never lost a night's sleep over a woman until you appeared. Last night I didn't sleep at all, and cold showers are not my scene. It has to stop.' He returned his attention to the road ahead. 'You demanded marriage, I'm giving it to you.'

'Just like that,' she said lightly. 'It would be simpler and cheaper to take a sleeping-pill.' She saw Alex's lips twitch in the hint of a smile.

'So practical, Saffron. But think of the fun I'd be missing,' he drawled suggestively.

'But you can't marry me...' she protested; she couldn't afford to seem too keen. She had to make him sweat...

'I can and I will,' He took one hand off the wheel again, picked up Saffron's and placed it cosily on his hard thigh. 'And there are other compensations. Mama will stop throwing women at me, for one. And I'll be forty next birthday; it's time I thought of an heir. A son to carry on after me,' he clarified firmly, then added with the hard cynicism that Saffron detested, 'If you were honest with yourself, though I know the concept is difficult for women to accept, you'd admit that I am giving you precisely what you have wanted from the first day you set eyes on me and grabbed me so dramatically before blushing coyly and batting those big green eyes of yours, sweetheart.'

'But I don't want to marry you simply to assuage your lust and provide an heir,' she said coolly, feeling anything but cool... Events were sweeping her along at an alarming pace, just when she had thought she had got her life in order again. Alex's unprecedented announcement and, worse, his arrogant assumption that she should fall at his feet in gratitude had made her change her mind, and his last comment only reinforced her determination to seek revenge. To suggest that she had been chasing him from the first day they met was so typically arrogant of him that she had to clench her hand into a fist to prevent herself thumping him.

'Would you rather I declared undying love?' He waited for her answer.

The silence lengthened as she searched for some frivolous response, but words failed her. 'Well...' For a man like Alex to fall in love was an impossibility, so why did the thought hurt, and why did her own reason for marrying him suddenly seem so revolting?

'Too late; you can't back out now. I fixed the special licence on the way to collect you this morning.'

'But surely I have to complete a form, birth date, that sort of thing?' she gabbled. It could not be that simple. Alex had proposed to her and she had accepted more or less by default. Her temper cooled and the doubts rushed in, setting her mind awhirl with a conflict of emotions, none very enviable.

'I had you investigated, remember.'

Saffron had forgotten about that and his reminder only served to fuel her desire for revenge.

'Out you get; we can walk the rest of the way.' He had parked the car in Hatton Garden, and before Saffron could gather her scattered wits she was being ushered into a diamond merchant's.

'Desmond is a partner and friend of mine. He deals in diamonds and precious stones, and keeps a small exclusive selection of special jewellery by a little-known Russian designer. I think you'll like what you see.'

She simply nodded, trying to disguise her wide-eyed wonder at her surroundings, fighting to appear the cool sophisticate. She sat on a comfortable settee with Alex beside her in what appeared to be a rather luxurious lounge; on a low table in front of them were displayed some of the most exquisite rings Saffron had ever seen in her life. In the chair opposite sat a man of about fifty—Desmond.

'I never thought Alex would marry, but, having met you, Saffron, I can see why he's taking the plunge.'

Before she could respond to the compliment Alex interrupted. 'She's mine, Desmond, so keep your flattery to yourself and show us the rings.'

'Mine'. Saffron heard the possessive tone in his voice and felt the sudden stiffening in his large body next to her own. She glanced up at him just as he looked down at her. Desmond said something neither of them heard as tension ignited the air between them. Saffron could not escape the burning intensity of Alex's gaze. Her lips parted in a small O of shock as she recognised the flare of desire in his dark eyes, and something more sinister—an assumption of ownership, ruthless and total.

What on earth was she doing here? Had she taken leave of her senses completely? She did not want a ring. She did not want to be within a thousand miles of Alex Statis. Her half-baked idea of revenge was futile. She had seen it in Alex's eyes, felt it in his touch. He would possess her completely. Eat her up and spit her out as so much garbage if she let him.

'Do you like this one?'

She looked down at where her hand lay in Alex's, wondering how it had got there. Then she gasped. Two white gold bands were held together every few millimetres with perfectly inset emeralds, the two bands twisting in the centre to form the mount for an exquisite blue-white diamond. It was unusual and intriguing and must cost a fortune. 'It's beautiful, but something smaller...' For a second she completely forgot that she was supposed to be taking the man for every penny she could get. She sucked in her breath as Alex tightened his grip on her hand.

'We will take it.' And, leaning over her, he covered her mouth with his own. She tried to freeze him out but he was not so easily discouraged; his teeth bit her bottom lip and her mouth opened to allow him access. She told herself she hated him, but as the kiss went on and on her resistance crumbled. When he finally lifted his head, she stared up at him, her green eyes dazed, her lips softly swollen. 'To a short but sweet engagement, my little witch,' he drawled throatily.

Saffron thought she smiled and agreed though she was past caring. She only wanted to get away somewhere on her own, anywhere, and try to make sense of her wildly fluctuating emotions. But she knew it would not be easy...

*   *   *

Later Saffron was to agonise over how on earth she had allowed it to happen. But for the next two days she went around in a daze, one moment determined to back out of the marriage, the next, with one arrogant or possessive comment from Alex, equally determined to go ahead with the wedding simply to teach the swine a lesson . . .

Anna didn't help Saffron's confused emotional state by suddenly turning into a model of bustling efficiency. The older woman insisted on taking Saffron shopping and to Saffron's horror she ended up with a white wedding gown. A slinky pleated skirt almost to her ankles with a shoe-string overdress in the finest chiffon, the style was slightly 1920s, but the price designer original. The head-dress was little more than a shaped swath of chiffon that bound her topknot of curls and floated down over her shoulder. She looked at her reflection and what she saw was a sophisticated bride with the eyes of a child. She had no argument against Anna's declaration that it was perfect for a summer wedding, though she hated the way it made her feel: a complete hypocrite.

Three days later at a simple civil ceremony, Alex standing tall and elegant at her side, her hand firmly clasped in his as the dignitary read the marriage service, Saffron heard Alex's deep, resonant, 'I will,' and wanted to run.

This had gone far enough. She opened her mouth to say no, but Alex, sensing her hesitation, tilted her chin with one finger. Her eyes widened in alarm at the blaze of emotion in his, and just for a second she thought she saw his eyes flash—a trace of pleading that was at once suppressed. How powerful, how proud he was, she thought, and in that instant her wildly vacillating emotions of the past few weeks vanished. Like a shutter lifting in her mind she suddenly recognised what she had feared and fought so long to deny. It hit her with the force of a nova star, shattering all her preconceived ideas of love and marriage...

She loved Alex. She hated what he was, but somehow she had fallen in love with him.

'Saffron,' he murmured, his eyes burning into hers, hypnotising her into submission.

'I will,' she said, the words trembling on her lips. Alex lifted her hand and slid a plain gold band on her finger.

'You belong to me now.' And his lips met hers in a devastating kiss, stamping on her his possession in front of the world.

The penthouse and pavilion suite of a top London hotel had been reserved for the reception. Cameras flashed as they arrived. The wedding announcement three days previously in *The Times* had caused a stir among the world's journalists. Alex Statis, the multi-millionaire, wedding an unknown. It was yet another reason why Saffron had continued with the charade of preparing for the wedding. Alex had called the papers before he had even told her, and his bullying tactics of the past few days had served to heighten her anger, while his passionate kisses and constant sensual touches had left her floundering in a sea of conflicting emotions she could not begin to decipher.

Talk and laughter echoed around the extravagantly mirrored walls of the elegant pavilion room that led out on to a wide balcony complete with fountain and waterfall and a stunning view over London. Later, in the sumptuously elegant dining-room, they ate excellent food and the champagne flowed freely. Desmond, as best man, made a humorous speech and Alex's acceptance was a masterpiece of wit.

Then Saffron was being congratulated by Anna and Aunt Katherina. She frowned thoughtfully as Maria murmured her congratulations, her green-eyed gaze resting on Anna and Katherina. Given Anna's story on the boat, it was surprising to see how well the sisters-in-law appeared to get along.

'Why the frown, darling? Tired?' Alex's husky voice whispered in her ear.

'No, no. I'm fine.'

'Pity; I want to take you to bed.' She forced herself to look up at him. He was devastatingly attractive in a pearl-grey suit, his dark eyes sparkling with laughter and something else she did not recognise. Just then Desmond made a great production of kissing the bride, although unfortunately he was hampered somewhat by the fact that Alex refused to remove his arm from around his bride's waist.

Saffron stood in the curve of her husband's arm and looked around the glittering throng. Alex was deep in conversation with Sylvia. The other woman had given Saffron one hate-filled glance and gritted congratulations before turning all her feminine charms on Alex. Saffron couldn't care less. She felt as if she was walking through a nightmare. How had she let it come to this? Her grief at Eve's death, her instant attraction to Alex and the discovery of who he really was had thrown her into an emotional minefield; torn between her attraction for Alex and her debt to her friend, her quick temper had done the rest.

A small sad smile twisted her lips as she acknowledged once more what she had been fighting for weeks. She loved Alex, and when she had made her vows it had not been because he had forced or intimidated her but because in her heart of hearts it was what she wanted. Hate and love walked a thin line, and in the throes of what was her first real sexual experience Saffron had managed to tangle the two completely, with devastating results.

She was married to a man she loved but should hate. She glanced at the crowd of smartly dressed guests. Not one of them was hers. She had tried to contact Tom and Vera, the couple she had lived with for the past few years, at Anna's instigation, but they had been away on holiday.

And how Eve would have loved to see this: a top hotel and the top people, and little Saffron Martin married to the catch of the year. She was completely out of her depth and going down for the third time.

She looked up at Alex, her stomach curling in nervous anticipation of the night ahead. Yet the warmth of his large strong hand at her waist was oddly comforting; she felt safe, something she had never experienced since the death of her parents.

Later, having changed into a smart buttercup-yellow suit, with a dramatic black camisole peeking through the jacket lapels, ridiculously high-heeled black court shoes and a black bag, Saffron left with Alex to journey to Paris.

Covered in rice and confetti, she slid into the Jaguar. Alex slipped in beside her, chuckling as he brushed a handful of rice from his thick black hair.

'Enough to feed a child in the Third World,' he remarked with a rueful smile.

'I doubt you worry much about the Third World,' Saffron snapped before she realised what she had done.

Alex started the car; they were driving to Heathrow where the Statis jet was waiting. Then he shot her a curious glance. 'You don't really know me very well, do you, Saffron?' he said softly.

She glanced at him and for an instant she thought she saw something in his brown eyes—a hint of vulnerability?—that made her heart inexplicably lurch in her chest, but quickly she dismissed the notion. She knew him far too well; that was the trouble...

'Not to worry, darling; we're almost there, and very shortly you will know me as intimately as it's possible to know another person. No more delaying tactics. Soon you will be mine utterly and completely,' Alex drawled hardly, his glance flicking over her slim form with a possessive male sensuality that brought a blush to her cheeks.

With hindsight she realised morosely that that was another reason why she had continued with her plan of revenge. On the day he had presented her with the engagement ring, they had shared a celebratory dinner at his apartment and Alex had deliberately set out to seduce her with a sensual sophistication that had had her blushing scarlet and her head spinning. It had taken all her self-control to prevent him bedding her there and then, until he had lost his cool and said, 'For God's sake, woman, we're engaged; I've bought you the obligatory rock to prove it. I've waited long enough. I want you now, damn it!'

His cynical mention of the engagement ring had been enough to have her stiffening in anger, remembering how many poor girls had been destroyed to satisfy his greed, and she had sworn again to have her revenge.

He had taken her home in a cold fury. She had hardly slept for the next few nights, and when she had finally got to sleep her dreams had been full of a naked, erotic Alex inexplicably entwined with Eve...

Saffron closed her eyes briefly as the aircraft took off, and cursed the circumstances and her own quick temper that had led her to this point. She turned her head slightly. Alex was pulling his tie from his strong throat and deftly unfastening the first couple of buttons of his white shirt. Feeling her eyes on him, he cast her a lazy glance.

'Formalities over; now for the best part.' His deep, sexy voice and easy smile sent warning signals through every nerve in her body. He leant closer, at the same time slipping off his jacket. 'Want to join the mile-high club, Mrs Statis?'

The sun's rays slanting through the window caught his profile, accentuating his rugged features and highlighting a few silver strands in his thick dark hair. He gave the impression of power and authority, and a raw male virility that held her gaze even against her will. Then he jiggled his eyebrows suggestively, and Saffron couldn't prevent a smile and a soft chuckle escaping her at his antics.

'Well?' he prompted, one long finger reaching to trace gently the outline of her mouth. He placed his other arm about her shoulder, urging her towards him. 'Tempted, wife?' he prompted again teasingly.

She was... Saffron wanted nothing more than to sink into his arms where she belonged. 'Wife', he had said, and with that one word Alex had opened her eyes to exactly what she had done. She had married the man she loved but could not respect. What hope was there for their future in such circumstances?

'There's no need to look so stricken, darling,' Alex said, the laughter dying from his eyes. 'I was only teasing.' His finger fell from her mouth to settle in the V of her jacket lapels, while his mouth gently grazed hers.

'The flight is barely an hour and the first time I get you in a bed I intend to keep you there for a week— probably longer!' he murmured against her lips. Then, straightening, he added, 'I have a suspicion that this ferocious physical need will not be assuaged so easily,' and grimaced as though he resented his desire for her.

Saffron knew exactly how he felt... his finger on her throat, the touch of his lips and she wanted him. 'I think I'll rest for a while,' she mumbled as Alex settled back in his seat although his arm remained around her shoulders.

'Do that—I don't want you tired later,' he drawled huskily.

Cowardly she closed her eyes, her thoughts too hard to face. She realised with blinding clarity that she had probably loved Alex from the first time they had been alone together on Mykonos, when she had accepted, to the lush strains of a Rossini overture, her own sensual nature while not realising that it was only Alex who had the power to make her feel that way. She had fallen into a trap of her own making, by denying him her body even after he had given her the engagement ring; he had charged ahead with the wedding simply to slake his physical lust.

She could not settle for that kind of marriage, even if she was foolish enough to try. It was doomed from the start because he was still the man who had shared ownership of Studio 96. Maybe he just owned the building and didn't know what was going on. But common sense told her she was simply searching for excuses for Alex. In her heart she knew she could never forget his past, so her love for him would have to end before it had even begun.

Looking back, she could see what a naïve idiot she had been. Alex had alternately teased and beguiled her on board the yacht, until she had admitted to herself her growing fascination for the man, only to have it destroyed first by her jealousy of the sophisticated Sylvia, and completely by her recognition of where she had seen Alex before.

Her growing love had turned to instant hate, and her red-headed temper had fuelled her asinine plan of revenge. Who was it who said 'Be careful of what you wish for in case you get it'? How true! But what was she going to do now? Unconsciously a deep, quavering sigh escaped her.

'Why the sigh?'

Saffron opened her eyes to find Alex gazing at her with tender intensity and she looked at him for a long moment, a tide of colour washing slowly up her cheeks at his obvious concern. 'I...'

She was saved by the arrival of a stunning blonde stewardess.

'Congratulations, Mr Statis. I never thought I'd see the day.'

Alex's attention was immediately on the tall blonde. 'Thank you, Eve; I didn't know you were back.'

Saffron watched his easy, familiar smile and the blonde's response, her heart freezing at the coincidence. Another Eve, but this one alive and well and obviously very well acquainted with Alex. It highlighted so poignantly her worst fear. She could not go ahead with the marriage and forget about her friend, burying her head in the sand like an ostrich, because there would always be something or someone, perhaps simply a name, to remind her of Alex's involvement in her friend's destruction. She could not live her life on a lie. She sipped the champagne provided and if she was quiet Alex did not seem to notice.

The light was fading when they arrived at the small exclusive hotel in Paris. 'I hope you don't mind, Saffron, but I've spent so much time away from work chasing you that I can only afford three days before I have to be back in the office. But don't worry, I'll make it up to you later.' Alex gave her hand a squeeze as they were shown to their suite. 'In a few months we'll take a long honeymoon cruising the Med or the West Indies, whatever you like.'

What she would have liked was to be anywhere in the world but here, she thought sadly, her gaze flickering around the room, barely taking in the opulent surroundings but studiously avoiding looking at Alex. She had not the slightest idea what she was going to do. In the taxi she had run through a dozen scenarios from

going ahead with the marriage, telling Alex the truth,
to faking a serious illness.

Her eyes alighted on a table set beside the lusciously
draped window. A massive arrangement of red roses was
the centrepiece, and there were two place-settings, the
finest crystal glasses and champagne in a free-standing
bucket at one side. 'We're dining here?' she burst out.
Somehow she had thought they would go out to dinner,
which would have given her more time, but obviously
Alex had other ideas.

'Where else on our honeymoon?' he husked, his arms
closing around her from behind, holding her tight against
his tall body, his lips nuzzling her neck. 'Alone at last.'
His breath singed her skin.

'What a cliché.' She tried to laugh and pulled herself
out of his arms. 'You order the food; I need to freshen
up.'

She dashed for the door she imagined was the
bathroom, and for the first time that day got something
right. She closed the door and bolted it, her heart
pounding, her mouth dry. In ordinary circumstances tonight could have been a dream come true: she was
married to the man she loved and on her honeymoon.
But she could not fool herself; it was hopeless . . .

God help her! She swallowed hard. What a mess! She
should have remembered; she had heard somewhere that
revenge was best taken cold, and given that she was
always hot around Alex her scheme would never have
worked anyway, never mind the fact that she had fallen
in love with him . . . She was only putting off the inevi-
table by hiding in the bathroom. She would have to go
for the truth and pray that Alex would understand. That
was if he didn't kill her first . . .

They did not linger over the meal. Saffron had no
appetite, and quaffed the champagne as if it were going
out of style, while she would have sworn, if she had not

known better, that Alex was nervous. They drank a toast to their marriage and Saffron invented a few others simply to delay the hour of reckoning, and amazingly he allowed her to get away with it. Finally however, he drained his glass, placed it quite deliberately on the table and stood up.

'I think we'll forgo coffee; you may use the bathroom first.' And, catching her hand, he pulled her to her feet and led her into the large bedroom.

Her green eyes widened at the sight of the huge bed that dominated the room. Tell him...tell him now...her mind screamed, but she had trouble tearing her gaze away. A frothy white négligé—a present from Anna— lay draped across the white lace cover, beside it a pair of black silk pyjamas. The intimacy of the nightwear brought home to her as nothing else exactly what she had done, and what she was inviting. For the first time in days fear cleared her head with remarkable alacrity.

'Alex, I've made a mistake.' The words were out before she could stop them. She straightened her shoulders and turned to face him. Truth was the only way. She tilted her head back to look up into his handsome face. 'I should never have married you.'

'Say that again.' He shook his head in disbelief, one lock of black hair falling over his broad forehead.

'I want to go back to England. We can get the marriage annulled and forget it ever happened,' she said in a tight, nervous voice. She turned and walked towards the door, but Alex's arm around her waist halted her, hauling her back against his hard body.

'You're nervous,' he said softly. His dark head bent and he nuzzled the soft line of her neck, but she pulled free, stepping away from him.

'No, I mean it.' She reached for the door-handle and was suddenly swept off her feet and into Alex's arms.

'Foolish girl. It's just natural bridal nerves. Hell, surprisingly enough, I'm nervous myself!'

If his words had been meant to reassure her they didn't. She struggled in his arms, crying out, 'I am not nervous, damn you! Put me down.' And he did, dropping her on the bed. She lay flat on her back staring up at him, trying to find the words to extricate herself from the mess she had made of everything.

'Sorry.' Inadequate, she knew. 'I really am sorry, Alex; I thought...' She paused then began to talk and could not stop. 'I thought I could marry you and hurt you the way you have hurt so many people by your determination to make money legally or otherwise. I wanted to make you suffer like my friend Eve. To take you for every penny I could get.'

But I realised I loved you, was what she wanted to say but couldn't, because the one thing she had recognised while she had been agonising over her marriage the last few hours was that Alex did not love her. His reasons for marrying her were not much better than Saffron's had been originally. Instead she added in a flat voice, 'You see, I know all about Studio 96.'

His dark head jerked back. 'You know Studio 96?' he rasped, his eyes narrowed on her pale face.

At least he had not attempted to deny it, Saffron thought dully, sitting up and swinging her legs over the side of the bed, her feet finding the floor. 'Yes, I know it.' She ran her small hands through her hair, brushing it back from her face, and glanced up at Alex, He was standing perfectly still as if carved in stone, his rugged face expressionless. 'I know you owned that disgusting massage parlour.' There; she had finally said it.

'I see, and were you an employee?' he ground out scathingly.

Saffron stared at him. 'I lasted exactly fifteen minutes, the length of time it took me to realise what kind of health club it was, and you, Alex, showed me the door. Unfortunately my best friend Eve was not so lucky. I lost touch with her and then a few months ago a policeman arrived at my door to tell me Eve had died of an overdose and left a letter for me. Working in that supposedly high-class health club had destroyed her, while men like you get rich on the proceeds.'

Her green eyes searched his face in puzzled frustration. 'Why, Alex? You have so many other business interests, why a sordid massage parlour?' She shook her head; it didn't make sense. 'Greed?' she queried, but did not really want to hear his response.

Confession was supposed to be good for the soul, but Saffron was having serious doubts. She stood up, and would have walked past Alex but he reached for her, his fingers digging cruelly into her arm. He spun her round, his other hand curved around her neck, and she raised her eyes to his, and what she saw made the blood freeze in her veins.

'Of course; the young platinum——' He stopped. He had finally recognised her from the past. Shaking his head as if to dispel some image, he carried on coldly, clinically, 'Am I to understand you married me today as some kind of revenge for the death of your friend, and now you want out? So what has changed your mind, Saffron, dearest?' he demanded with chilling cynicism. 'The thought of sleeping with me too much for you to stomach?' he ended in a snarl.

'I... No...' She didn't know what to say; his hand was curved around her throat, his black eyes glittered with an unholy light, and for a second she feared for her life.

'My sweet Saffron, the epitome of all innocence, and more Greek than I when it comes to revenge.' A harsh laugh escaped him as his hand moved under her chin, forcing her head back. His glittering gaze clashed with hers. 'Tell me, you bitch, when did you decide on this plan of yours—the minute we met or before? Is that why you worked for my mother?'

'No—no—I...' Saffron was petrified. Alex's hand slid from her arm to curve around her waist, holding her manacled to the hard, muscular length of his body. His hand at her chin was hurting her jawbone, and the icy fury in his· eyes, the harshly forbidding expression on his ruthless face made her want to cry out in terror.

'Answer me,' he grated.

'I—I didn't recognise you until we left the yacht. The business suit, navy... Before, I thought I knew you but the suit and briefcase... I realised who you were and ha——' She almost said 'hated you' but stopped herself in time. She was alone in the bedroom with a furiously angry male. This was not going at all as she had hoped. How idiotic of her to expect that a man like Alex would let her just walk away. She must have been out of her tiny mind... But then it felt as if she had been in that state ever since she'd clapped eyes on the damn man! she thought helplessly.

'Hated me? Then I think I should give you reason.' His pitiless intention was obvious, and even as Saffron tried to struggle she was once more on the bed, but this time Alex was beside her.

CHAPTER SEVEN

'NO, ALEX, you don't understand. I changed my mind.
I should...' Her words were stilled by his mouth covering
hers in a bitter parody of a lover's kiss. When it was
over she lay panting on the bed, his strong body half
covering hers as he swiftly removed her jacket and dis-
pensed with her skirt with ruthless efficiency.

'Understand? I understand too damn well, you little
cheat. "I changed my mind"?' he mimicked scathingly,
and all the time his gaze never left her face, until she
was half demented by the probing black eyes which
seemed intent on devouring her. 'I hate to tell you,
darling, but you don't have that choice,' he grated with
seething sarcasm, the straps of her camisole snapping
like matchsticks as he tore the garment from her body,
exposing her naked breasts to the brightly lit room. 'Yes,
Alex, please, Alex,' he sneered. 'I'll have you begging
for it, you little bitch.'

But the cold fury in his voice, his tight mouth, the
dull flush on his high cheekbones revealed the massive
effort he was exerting to gain self-control and not to
take her there and then.

Perspiration broke out on her temples. 'No, please...'
But her plea fell on deaf ears as she tried to struggle,
lashing out at him with feet and hands, her efforts
fruitless because he was so much larger and rage lent
him added purpose.

'You're sorry?' he snarled. 'You want to leave?' He
slid off the bed but kept her pinned to the mattress with
one large hand in the middle of her chest; with the other

116

he removed the rest of his clothes, carelessly throwing them to the floor. 'I'll show you sorry, Saffron,' he vowed ruthlessly, his black eyes roaming over her face and almost naked, trembling form with lascivious intent.

'You can't be serious,' she cried inanely. He towered over her, his nude body gleaming golden in the artificial light, and to her horror a blush ran from her head to her toes. He was so beautifully male that even in her terror she still reacted to him.

'I have never been more serious in my life.' He joined her on the bed and she kicked out at him, but one hard thigh quickly trapped her flailing limbs.

'Did you really think you could get revenge on a Greek? We are past masters at the art. You should have remembered that, Saffron.' He rolled over on top of her and, catching her hands, held them pinned to the pillow above her head in one of his, his full weight pressing the breath from her body, but still she shivered at the intimate brush of his mat of chest hair against her naked flesh.

She bucked against him in a vain attempt to dislodge him. 'Get off me, you great hulking brute. I hate you!' Her quick temper and sheer terror made her strike at him with anything she could think of. 'My God, you and your Greek heritage! Family! What a laugh! Even your own mother is afraid of you; for years you've made her suffer with relatives she can't abide.'

If she'd thought he was angry before, that was nothing compared to his reaction now...

Alex's head jerked back and he stared down at her in violent black fury, his eyes flaming with rage. His grip tightened on her wrists, forcing a low cry from her. 'Wrong move, Saffron,' he grated between his teeth, his dark head bending lower, and Saffron felt herself begin to tremble. 'You will not distract me with wild accusations. I intend having you, and you must have realised by now that I usually get what I want in the end.'

'However low you have to stoop to do it?' she cried unwisely, but fear and anger mingled with sheer panic made her forget all caution. 'About what I would have expected from a man no better than a pimp,' she added, dredging up a last few grains of defiance.

He did not notice her panic, only the derision in her words. 'Don't ever, *ever* call me that again if you value your life!' he snarled, and his hand reached out to tangle in her hair, jerking her head up towards him, his face only inches from her own. For a long moment he stared into her glittering angry eyes, a muscle jerking in his cheek.

'The truth hurts,' she managed to fight back.

'You are either a fool or a very brave woman,' he snarled, like a tiger about to pounce.

She looked at him with bitter resentment. As far as Alex was concerned she was a fool; she had known she was beaten from that day on Mykonos only she'd had too much pride and been too afraid to admit it.

His mouth fastened on hers brutally, kissing her with savage fury, and she moaned in pain and, more humiliatingly, aching longing. Sensing her reluctant response, his lips gentled, his mouth searched hers and his long fingers tightened their hold on her.

His breath seared her mouth and down the vulnerable curve of her throat. 'You are going to give me what I have paid for, my sweet wife.' He looked at her, his lips curved in a deadly smile, then his head lowered to her breast.

'I'm not...' she choked almost incoherently as his teeth bit lightly at her breast; he blatantly watched the nipple swell and tighten and then glanced knowingly up at her flushed face.

'You will, but don't worry—I won't take anything you aren't prepared to give.' His breathing had deepened but he spoke with a deadly calm that was more terrifying than his earlier rage. 'You have led me a merry dance. No woman has ever succeeded in doing that to me, and neither will you.'

Her heart racing, Saffron realised it was the devil in him talking, the powerful, cynical businessman against whom she had never stood a chance and whom she had been the biggest fool in Christendom even to try to outwit. Already she could feel a sweet tide of pleasure she couldn't resist flowing through her veins, and as his head lowered again, his tongue flicking lightly over the tip of her breast, she gasped and felt her body yielding itself to him in trembling anticipation, his to do with as he wanted, even as her mind tried to deny the ease with which he aroused her. She flinched as he raised his head to watch her.

'I did not mean to bite. There; I've kissed you better,' he said silkily, his free hand covering her other breast and squeezing gently. Saffron arched beneath him in helpless response, and his black eyes held hers, a glint of mockery in their fiery depths.

'It is time to pay the piper,' he rasped as his mouth claimed hers once more. For a second she offered a token resistance, clenching her teeth, but it did not last. His long, supple fingers played with the hard tip of her breast and her lips parted on a low moan, giving him the access he sought.

His kiss hardened, his tongue dancing in and out of every moist, secret corner of her mouth, while his hand taunted and teased, stroking down over her belly and beneath her briefs and garter belt, her only remaining clothes, to the soft red hair at the juncture of her thighs.

'Stockings. My favourite,' Alex said, kissing her navel. 'Hardly virginal,' he mocked, glancing up at her glazed eyes. 'Another little ruse, no doubt,' he grated as with slow deliberation he peeled her panties and stockings from her legs, kissing his way down and back up their shapely length, then once more finding her mouth.

Saffron knew she should fight, but had no will left; the blood pounded thick and hot through her veins, every nerve pulled taut with passion. Alex was an expert lover and his touch, the scent of him, the brush of skin on skin, the subtle play of his long fingers over her quivering, aching flesh melted her bones. He was so large, so powerful; the scent of him filled her nostrils and his touch filled her mind and heart to the exclusion of all else.

She was not aware that he had freed her hands until she felt the strength of his broad shoulders beneath her fingertips. She began caressing him in urgent need. Her lips parted and she whimpered as she felt the steel-hard weight of him against her thigh, while with mouth and tongue he teased and tormented her, kissing every inch of her soft flesh.

'Saffron, my spicy Saffron,' he growled as he showered kisses back down her stomach, trailing his hands over her burgeoning breasts and down. He nudged her legs apart with one hard-muscled thigh then trailed kisses along her hipbone, and she cried out as his wicked fingers delved in the heart of her womanhood and his kiss became too intimate to endure.

Soon she was twisting and gasping, her hands clenching the sheet as her body arched in a bow, seeking, needing only the fulfilment that Alex could give her.

Suddenly he was over her again, his broad chest hard against her breast. His mouth moved insistently over hers with renewed passion, ravaging in its ruthless possession. She felt a brief flare of panic as he swiftly urged her legs wider apart and slid between them. She stiffened slightly but he was having none of it. His large hands curved under her buttocks and lifted her from the bed as he came down, letting her take his whole weight as he moved fiercely into her in one driving thrust...

She cried out with the pain and Alex reared back. She looked straight into his eyes, and for a second she thought she registered regret, then his head lowered, his lips took hers in a strangely soothing, achingly tender kiss and amazingly she was no longer hurting, her slender sheath clenching around his rigid, pulsing length.

'Yes, yes!' he encouraged hoarsely. 'I won't hurt you again. Relax,' he breathed into her open mouth. One strong hand supporting his weight, he curved the other up her back and around her shoulder, still joined but rocking her in his embrace. 'That's it, my little witch; go with it.' As he spoke he eased her back down and moved slowly inside her, his head bent to kiss her in a long, hot, open-mouthed kiss, his tongue following the rhythm of their bodies.

Saffron gasped as she felt her body absorbing and adjusting to Alex's, then cried out as the slow, lazy rhythm picked up speed, his hardness filling her until she cried out again, frightened by her own fervent response. Her small hands curved around and up his back, her fingers digging into his satin-smooth skin, her legs instinctively lifting, clamping high around his waist. She closed her eyes tight, her body clenching in what seemed like anguished pain as Alex, dark and all-powerful, swept her into a maelstrom of feelings and sensations she had never imagined possible. Her body finally convulsed in a shattering climax that went on and on, in wave after wave of storming ecstasy.

Then Alex, with a 'God!' groaned out in a hoarse, breathless sigh, shuddered, his huge body going rigid, before he collapsed on top of her, his heartbeat racing with hers, and he trembled, as Saffron did, for long moments afterwards.

Eventually Saffron, the fires which had consumed her slowly dying down, felt a curious exhaustion, and an emptiness in her heart that brought moisture to her eyes. Alex rolled off her and lay flat on his back, an arm thrown over his eyes, his mighty chest still heaving. The rasping sound of his breathing was the only noise in the brightly lit room. She glanced sideways at him and quickly away, the lengthening silence a testimony to the chasm that lay between them even when they had been as intimate as it was possible for two people to be.

With a choked sob, she slid off the bed and stumbled towards the bathroom. She was surprised but strangely unconcerned when Alex followed her, curving his arm around her waist.

'Allow me.' She stood motionless in his hold as he turned on the taps and they both watched the large bath slowly fill. 'Are you all right?' he asked tersely, lifting her in his arms and depositing her gently in the warm water.

'Of course,' she murmured. They were talking like two strangers, stilted and polite. But Alex was a stranger to her, she thought with sad irony. Now she knew his body, but the man ... villain or virtuous? ... she would never know, and—please, God!—that fact alone would some day kill this hopeless love she felt for him, and set her free.

Closing her eyes, she lay back; she was so tired and heartsore, she didn't want to think. She felt the gentle touch of the sponge as Alex carefully bathed her but was too exhausted to object.

Later he lifted her out, dried her tender flesh with a large white towel and then, with a rare gentleness, carried her back to the bed again. Reaction setting in, she lay like a rag doll as he covered her with the white sheet. For a second she felt his hand tremble against her cheek, but she must have imagined it as she opened her eyes to stare up into a dark face blank of all expression.

'Go to sleep; we will talk in the morning.'

Her eyelids suddenly seemed too heavy to keep open and, with a shuddering sigh, she fell asleep.

Saffron sighed, and snuggled closer into the enveloping warmth of the hard male body; the steady, rhythmic beat beneath her ear filled her with a deep sense of security and, drifting in the no man's land between sleep and wakefulness, she luxuriated in the rare feeling of utter contentment.

Her lashes flickered against the soft curve of her cheek and she stirred restlessly, reluctant to leave her safe cocoon of peace. Then memory returned and her eyes flashed open. She blinked once, twice. The room was lit with the early morning rays of the sun, the curtains open, the sound of traffic bringing her to full consciousness.

A heavy weight pinned her to the bed, and she carefully looked down at the arm that lay across her waist, and lower to the thigh that anchored her legs. Alex! Slowly her eyes trailed up over a male hip, waist and shoulder until she met the dark, inscrutable gaze of her husband.

'Awake at last,' he murmured softly. He was lying on his side, his elbow on the pillow to prop his head, and his eyes gleamed mockingly down at her as she tried to wriggle free from beneath his arm and leg. 'Why the hurry, Saffron? You aren't going anywhere.'

'I want to get up.'

'So do I—oh, so do I,' he chuckled.

Saffron felt the stirring of his arousal against her hip and blushed scarlet, but could not repress a shiver of reaction as he slowly and deliberately slid his hand from her waist up over her breast, throat, and to her face. He smoothed her tangled mass of red hair from her brow and, sliding his fingers through the glittering strands, spread them across the pillow.

'What time is it?' she croaked.

'Six. Plenty of time.' Alex's hand slid back down over her throat, his fingers lingering on the soft hollows. 'Last night I wanted to kill you.' His hand tightened for a second on her neck.

'No need—I'm leaving,' Saffron said, tension making her words sound harsh. Alex was too close, too over-powering and she had to get away.

As if she had never spoken he continued, 'But this morning I have a much better plan.' His hand resumed its downward journey and brushed the rosy peak of one breast then, with clever fingers, manipulated the tip to pebble-hardness.

'No.' She was protesting against both his plan and the sensual intent she saw in his dark, slumberous eyes.

'But you have not heard my plan, Saffron, my sweet,' he mocked softly, his fingers teasingly walking across to her other breast. 'I will not allow you to leave me; you can forget it. But you wanted revenge. I am half Greek; I can understand that and so you shall have it. You can spend my money how you like.' His thumb brushed back and forward over her pouting nipple, and she bit her lip to keep down the low moan of pleasure.

'I'm a reasonable man; last night I lost my temper a little, but after careful consideration nothing has changed. We both had our own reasons for this mar-riage. I thought yours was money, and all you have really done is prove me right.'

He sounded so cool, so sensible, and there was a hor-rible kind of truth in Alex's words that made Saffron cringe even as her pulse-rate leapt at his wandering hands.

'And I shall have my heir and you to play with, sweet Saffron. Whenever, however, wherever I feel like!'

She looked at him nervously, her body already responding to the promise of his, and as she loved him so she hated him for rendering her so helpless. She had not missed the threat in his words. She felt his hard thigh press down on her slender legs and, with one arm trapped under Alex's body, she was at a hopeless disadvantage, but with her free hand she clasped his wrist, trying to stop the torment he was inflicting on her swollen breasts. 'Stop.' But he simply dragged her hand with his.

'I might stop some day.' His dark eyes gleamed with sardonic amusement. 'But certainly not today, and if you were honest you would admit you don't want me to.'

Saffron glared at him bitterly; the fiend was right and he knew it. She dug her nails into the underside of his wrist, hoping to hurt him and get him to stop.

Instead one dark eyebrow rose and his lips thinned as he unhurriedly used the hand that was propping his head to catch hers and force it over the top of her head. 'Now what, Saffron?' he mocked silkily.

She shivered as his free hand returned to tormenting her swollen breasts and her green eyes, sparkling with a mixture of anger and arousal, clashed with his. 'Don't do that.' She tried to twist away from him but it was a futile gesture. Alex, stretched out beside her, his rugged face looming over her, the early morning stubble casting a shadow over his square jaw, was obviously enjoying her discomfort; it was there in the cynically smiling mouth and his cool, assessing brown eyes fixed firmly on her flushed face.

'I said anytime anywhere—my choice,' he reiterated with deadly determination. 'My money, my plaything,' he murmured as he bent his head.

She was trapped, spread out before him, one hand still under his body, the other forced over her head and pinned to the pillow, while he moved his heavy thigh lightly up and down her lower body, and his free hand took impossible liberties with her tender flesh as his mouth sought hers in a slow burning kiss that built into a ravishment of her senses. She trembled as heat gathered in her loins, and his mouth suddenly dropped to her breast and began to suckle on the rigid tip.

Saffron gasped and arched at the same time as Alex's leg forced hers apart and his long, tactile fingers slid between the secret soft folds of her feminine flesh, finding the pulsing sweet centre of her desire. 'Please—you can't,' she murmured in anguish, torn between the delicious delight of his mouth and hands and the humiliation at her weakness.

But Alex simply moved from one breast, his black eyes flashing triumphantly to her face, and resumed suckling its partner, while his hand kept up an insistent teasing, tantalising rhythm. She felt her muscles clench, her body lifting, yielding to the demands of her own sexuality and Alex's sensual mastery. She closed her eyes, her face taut with pleasure, as Alex increased his rhythmic caress and the pressure of his mouth on her breasts.

'Please—oh, please!' she cried as her body trembled on the pinnacle of relief, and then clenched in a convulsive surrender.

The shuddering tremors stopped and Saffron finally opened her eyes. Alex had slipped an arm around her shoulder and his other hand rested lightly on the soft nest of red curls at the juncture of her thighs. She flushed scarlet as she met his dark, enigmatic gaze, shocked at his manipulation of her body, but more confused than anything. 'Why did...?' She couldn't continue.

He kissed her damp forehead, and smiled, a long, slow, completely masculine grin. 'Proving a point, maybe. You're mine to do what I like with.'

Tears of utter humiliation hazed her green eyes, but she refused to give in to them. She glanced down his long, naked body. 'Humiliating me doesn't do much for you, though, does it?' she retaliated, aware of his aroused state.

Reaching out his hand, he tilted her chin, his eyes dark and oddly intent. 'Maybe pleasuring you was all I intended.'

Saffron's eyes widened in surprise and puzzlement. 'Degrading me, you mean.'

'Don't look so shocked, Saffron; it's very flattering for a man to know he can please his woman in many ways, and nothing that brings pleasure between a husband and wife is degrading, you little innocent.'

His husky chuckle only fuelled Saffron's bitter humiliation. She tried to twist out of his arms, but he held her fast.

'Surprisingly, last night you were a virgin, and maybe I was less than gentle,' he admitted. His dark eyes caught and held hers as his hand, at the nape of her neck, kept her face towards his. 'You must be sore after last night; maybe this morning I was simply being considerate.'

Alex, considerate? The mind boggled, Saffron thought sadly, and closed her eyes, wishing she could shut out Alex and her love for him as easily.

'Come on, Saffron, get up,' he commanded softly. She opened her eyes, and he was standing leaning over her, a slight smile quirking the edges of his finely chiselled mouth. 'I need a cold shower and you need to pack; we're leaving in a couple of hours.'

'What?' she queried, momentarily fascinated by the length of his thick dark lashes curving over his half-closed eyes, successfully masking his expression. No man should have eyelashes like that; it was sinful.

'Pack—Saffron—we—are—leaving...' Alex said each word deliberately as though speaking to a child, his dark eyes gleaming with amusement as hers widened in shock.

'Why? Where are we going?' she asked, gathering her scattered wits. She had not given up hope of running back to England and forgetting the last disastrous and traumatic twenty-four hours, but that hope vanished as Alex straightened, all trace of amusement gone from his expression.

He stood, tall and naked but completely at ease with his nudity, as he levelled her with a hard glance. 'I am not such a fool as to give you a chance to run away, Saffron. I told you my terms; you work for your money with me,' he said starkly, his eyes hardening. 'We are going to Serendipidos where I can be assured of your safety.' One eyebrow slanted as he added silkily, 'And make sure you keep to our bargain, at least until I decide otherwise.'

She had no choice. Her heart-searching of yesterday, her conclusion that honesty was the best policy and all that, her reliance on the truth, had led her to this, she realised bitterly. If she had kept her mouth shut about the health club, if she had simply accepted what Alex had offered, and been prepared to forget his ignoble past, perhaps their marriage would have stood a chance. But now she was stuck with a husband who did not trust her, actively disliked her, and intended to keep her a virtual prisoner. A plaything to assuage his lust, and present him with an heir, his until he tired of her... 'Damn, damn, damn,' she swore.

Alex shot her a wry glance. 'Damning me won't help you, sweetheart.' And, turning, he strode off to the adjoining bathroom.

Saffron picked up the pillow and threw it after him, but it was wasted effort as it fell unnoticed and harmlessly against the closed door.

At the airport, Alex led her towards the private jet, parked some way away from the commercial flights, his strong fingers curved around her elbow, denying her any chance of a last-minute dash for freedom. He had never let her out of his sight for the past three hours, and she hoped it was not a foretaste of what was to follow.

The trouble was, she realised hopelessly, Alex had it all. The jet was simply a symbol of his success. She had heard a lot about him from his mother in the past few days; as a businessman and financier his success and wealth were apparently legendary, and Saffron, poor fool that she was, had had to go and fall in love with him.

If she had been thinking straight she might have realised the incongruity of Alex profiting from a massage parlour, but it did not occur to her until much later...

She allowed herself to be seated and barely noticed as Alex fastened her seatbelt. He must never know she loved him! That much she sadly recognised. He had married her for basically sensible reasons: lust and an heir. He did not believe in love and it would be the ultimate humiliation if he ever discovered how she really felt about him.

'Comfortable?' Alex's voice intruded on her worrying thoughts. She turned slightly, her glance skating over the proud head and hard features to rest on where his hands were deftly opening the briefcase on his lap.

'Yes, thank you,' she said politely.

'Good. I have work to do.' He wasn't even looking at her; she was already dismissed, his whole attention on the file he had taken from the briefcase.

'Plaything', he had said, and obviously meant, Saffron thought bitterly, and wondered how long she could stand the situation.

They left the plane at Athens and transferred to the helicopter, and twenty minutes later Saffron had her first view of Serendipidos.

'Your new home, Saffron; what do you think?' Alex queried, his deep voice sounding strangely remote through the headphones they were both wearing to cut out the noise of the helicopter.

She gazed out of the window at the panoramic view beneath. The blue-green sea, clear as crystal, broke into white horses around a tiny crescent-shaped island that rose steeply in the middle. It was no more than a mile square, if that; a wooden jetty stuck out like a black finger into the bay, and there were a few houses, hardly enough to call a village, and a winding white road that meandered in ever decreasing loops to the top of the hill above the bay.

'Beautiful,' she murmured appreciatively, then gasped as the helicopter circled a magnificent, long, low white villa overlooking the sea and surrounded on three sides by a high wall. In the enclosure she had a fleeting impression of gardens and terraces a riot of colour, saw the sun glinting off an oval swimming-pool, and then they were landing on the concrete pad at the rear of the house.

'I like to think so,' Alex responded to her comment, his smile one of sardonic amusement as, helping her to the ground, he added, 'And it is very private; the only way in or out is by helicopter or boat. Everything we need I have flown in. The relatives stay every year for a month or so, but most of the time we will be alone.'

'How long are we staying?' Saffron asked nervously, her agile mind very quickly digesting the fact that the island would not be easy to escape from.

'As long as it takes,' Alex murmured enigmatically, then strode towards the small dark woman rushing to meet him from the rear of the house.

As long as what takes? Saffron thought, trudging along behind him, the heat of the midday sun hitting her like a blowtorch. She was not in the least surprised that Alex no longer felt it necessary to lead her around by the arm; the arrogant oaf knew very well there was nowhere she could run to.

She stopped and watched him greet the elderly lady with a bear hug, and then shake hands with a surprisingly wizened old man whose currant-black eyes looked past Alex to where Saffron stood. His face split in an ear-to-ear grin then he said something in Greek that made Alex fling his head back and burst out laughing.

For a second Saffron was stunned by the sight of Alex, tall and casually dressed in cream trousers and a soft blue shirt, his darkly attractive face lit with laughter, the sun glinting off his night-black hair. He looked so handsome and carefree, and she felt her heart squeeze with longing for what might have been.

Introductions were over in a trice. The housekeeper and her husband, Despina and Georgos were all smiles as they led the way into the welcoming coolness of the house.

'What did Georgos say to make you laugh?' she asked as Alex ushered her into the main living-room with a hand on her back.

'Male joke; I doubt you would appreciate it.' And to her amazement he leaned towards her and kissed her slightly parted lips with a thoroughness that made her go weak at the knees. 'Come on, I'll show you around my home.'

'And my prison,' she shot back, more angry with herself because of her helpless reaction to his kiss than with him.

'It will be a prison of your own making, if you insist on being childish,' he said drily.

The house was lovely; Saffron could not pretend otherwise. The living-room and dining-room, family-room, study and kitchen all opened on to the garden and the sea but were connected by a long, wide, curving hall at the end of which an elegant marble staircase led to the upper floor.

'The hall was designed to be used as a reception area when I hold parties, or there are a lot of guests. It allows the rest of the family-rooms to be a more manageable size,' Alex informed her. 'More cosy.'

'You're hardly the cosy type,' Saffron snapped back.

He reached out and took hold of her chin, lifting it so that she had no option but to look at him. 'You will find out just what type I can be, if I have to put up with any more of your backchat, and I can promise you you will not like it.'

Her gaze was trapped by his, and she fought back the angry retort that hovered on her lips. His only visible sign of anger was the darkening glitter in his deep brown eyes, but she sensed the tension, the leashed strength, in his large body, and fear made her swallow her words.

'That's better, Saffron. You're learning,' he mocked, aware of her battle for control. Pulling her into his arms, he continued, 'Neither of us has got exactly what we expected from this union, but there's no reason why we can't behave like civilised adults.'

His knowing smile held no humour, and sent shivers of apprehension down her spine. 'No.' She drew a deep breath; held in his embrace she was much too vulnerable. The musky male scent of him, the warmth of his body undermined her self-control.

His eyes narrowed faintly as they travelled over her flushed, mutinous face. 'You are my wife and I am master in my own home. You will do as I say, and show respect to the staff, and that way we will get along just fine. Agreed?'

His grip tightened around her waist, his head bent and deliberately his breath feathered her cheek. 'Agreed?' he repeated hardly.

'Yes, yes,' she answered quickly, seconds before he kissed her thoroughly, declaring her his possession.

CHAPTER EIGHT

SUBDUED, Saffron followed Alex upstairs and into the master bedroom. She gazed around, her eyes widening in awe at the splendour before her. A huge bed on a raised dais dominated the room, the coverlet a work of art in white handmade lace, the headboard a swan with wings unfurled and incorporating side-tables, lights and what looked like a computer console. The floor was finely polished marble in a stunning white streaked with pink.

A door was standing half-open to one side and she had a brief glimpse of an equally extravagant bathroom. On the other side was another door which she imagined must lead to a dressing-room as there were no wardrobes in the bedroom, only an exquisite dressing-table, a casual arrangement of two long satin-covered sofas and an oval crystal and gold low table—minimal furniture but effective.

She turned and walked towards the large expanse of glass at the far end of the room and the balcony beckoning beyond. She slid open the door and stepped out; the heat hit her once again but she barely noticed as her green eyes filled with wonder at the view before her.

The gardens stretched out, gently sloping for about two hundred yards, and then fell away in a riot of colour, terrace upon terrace, to end on a beach of silver sand, washed by an azure sea. To the left she could just see the end of the jetty and the roofs of a few houses; to the right was simply more sand and sea, and then a sharp black cliff-face.

'It looks absolutely beautiful, and so quiet, so peaceful,' she murmured, almost to herself.

Alex had come up behind her and his arms slid around her waist, drawing her back against him, one hand holding her firm while his other slid up to cover her breast through the soft silk of the blouse she had teamed with matching cream silk trousers for travelling.

A quivering awareness darted through her as he nudged aside her long hair, his mouth sucking gently on the soft curve of her neck and then tracing up to her small ear.

'Beautiful! So are you, my sweet Saffron; pity the peace and quiet does not also apply to you.' He chuckled as his fingers found the waistband of her trousers and deftly unfastened the button, slipping down the zip, splaying out over her flat stomach. 'Come to bed,' he prompted throatily, his tongue licking gently around her ear as his other hand gently palmed her breast. 'Siesta, hmm?'

Saffron closed her eyes and bit down hard on her lip, trying to fight down the rising tide of desire that his touch evoked.

'You know you want to; why deny yourself?' Alex turned her in his arms. 'And me.' She felt his need against her belly, and hated the conflicting emotions that assailed her.

He was right, as usual, and with a low moan, half need and half despair, she curved her slender arms around his neck, urging his head down to her waiting lips.

That afternoon set the pattern for the weeks to come, though if Saffron had guessed what was to follow she would have fought harder to resist...

* * *

Saffron walked out of the sea, brushing her hair from her eyes, and ran across the beach to the shade of a large overhanging rock where she had left her towel. It was September now and the temperature was still in the hundreds, unseasonably hot; the only sensible place to be was in an air-conditioned room, but she could stand the silence of the villa no longer and, donning a brief black bikini, had ventured out in the afternoon sun.

Collapsing on the towel, her breathing heavy—she had swum longer and further than she should have—she rolled over on to her stomach and laid her head on her arms. She glanced along the deserted beach to the small huddle of houses and jetty and wondered for the millionth time how she was going to get away, or if she even wanted to...

From the first day on the island, when, in the middle of the afternoon, she had found herself on the large raised bed with Alex, who had conducted a relentless assault on her senses with a devilish expertise that had her crying out in ecstatic fulfilment, and then sunk in the depths of despair at her own degrading surrender, she had alternated between heaven and hell.

Over the weeks that had followed, she had begun to realise that the satiation which she had thought would follow quickly, and then she would be immune to him, was not about to happen. Instead, every night in the big bed she fell deeper and deeper under Alex's spell. He led her through the paths of the perfumed garden of eroticism with a hungry delight that encouraged her own surprisingly sensual nature to respond in kind. Together they found new and wondrous ways of pleasing each other until quite often the light of dawn threaded the sky before they fell into exhausted sleep.

It should have brought them closer together, but the reverse was true. In the first couple of weeks Alex had taken her shopping and to dinner in Athens a few times. She now had a wardrobe a film star would be proud of, and a diamond bracelet, and earrings to match her stunning engagement ring. Alex was lavish with money, and would not allow her to refuse whatever he offered, simply reminding her that she had married him for money, which in a way she had.

It was her own stupid fault that she had recognised that she loved him on her wedding-day and even more foolishly told him her ulterior motive for marrying him. Now she dared not tell him the truth. Instead she fought with him almost constantly. Thank God the house was isolated, otherwise everyone for miles around could hear their verbal sparring matches. As it was, Despina let her disapproval be known, even though she barely spoke English.

They had had one good day out, Saffron mused. The day he had taken her to explore the sights of Athens— the Acropolis, the Parthenon, and the ruins of the ancient theatre of Dionysus, which she had marvelled at. Then, later in the evening, when the sky was black, they had sat in the open-air theatre high above the Acropolis and watched in awe the sound and light show which illuminated the mighty Acropolis while the history of the city was told on tape by actors such as Richard Burton.

But over the past few weeks they had grown further and further apart. Saffron had not been off the island for six weeks. Alex, on the other hand, was rarely around. Every morning at eight the helicopter whisked him into his office in Athens, returning later and later at night as the weeks passed by. Last weekend he had not returned to the island at all; leaving a brief message with Despina, he had not spoken to Saffron, and had returned last night with no explanation.

Saffron had thought she was lonely before. An orphan, always on the outside looking in. But at least she had had her work her plans and ambition to comfort her. Now she was beginning to realise what true loneliness was.

She rubbed her hand idly across the moisture hazing her lovely eyes, The fact that Despina and Georgos spoke very little English did not help; she had tried walking to the jetty, but one bar, strictly for men, and a couple of houses did not make for a lively social life. A few smiles and a courteous Greek greeting and that was it. In desperation she had tried to offer Despina a make-up session and massage but had been greeted with a giggle and a no. Saffron honestly did not know how much more of this enforced idleness and brief, superficial conversations, or blazing rows with Alex, she could stand without going crazy.

Alex had arrived home after dinner last night and said curtly, 'I had a call from Mama today. She will be arriving on Friday, as will Aunt Katherina and Maria; arrange it with Despina, will you?'

Saffron, relaxing on the sofa, her legs curled under her, had looked up at Alex's entrance, and realised she had missed him. 'How?' she'd sneered mockingly. 'Sign language?' He strolled in at eleven at night without so much as an explanation and immediately began issuing orders. He was a pig...

'Cut out the sarcasm, Saffron; I'm not in the mood. I've had a hard few days.'

She had not seen him for three days, and he did looked tired; his tanned face had a greyish tinge, emphasising his rugged features. 'Have you had dinner? I could make you something.'

'I'm tired, not hungry.'

'Then go to bed.'

A grim smile tugged the corners of his hard mouth. 'Is that an invitation?' he demanded with a short, mocking laugh. 'My, we are getting bold.' And he bent over her to kiss her long and hard.

'No—no, it wasn't,' she spluttered, jumping to her feet.

'Sit down. I need a drink.' Alex walked to the array of bottles displayed on a long sideboard and poured a hefty shot of whisky into a crystal glass. He looked back over his shoulder, his dark eyes meeting hers. 'Join me in a nightcap?'

Saffron sank back down on the sofa. 'Yes, please— a small brandy and soda.'

Alex fixed the drink and handed it to her, the brush of his fingers against her own sending a too familiar tingle through her flesh. 'Thank you,' she said stiltedly, and took a swift swallow of her drink. Alex sat down beside her on the sofa, stretching the muscled length of his legs elegantly out in front of him, his head dropping back against the soft cushions, and drained his glass in one long swallow.

'I needed that. And now we need to talk.' His dark head turned slightly to the side so that he could study Saffron's delicate profile.

'What about?' she queried, shooting him a bitter glance. 'We said it all on our wedding night, I would have thought.'

'Not about us; that's not important,' he dismissed lazily, almost insolently. 'About the weekend. I do not want my mother or aunt or any other guests that may arrive upset in any way.' His hand reached out along the back of the sofa and tangled in Saffron's hair, turning her head towards him. 'In other words, Saffron, my sweet, I expect—no, demand that you keep control of that fiery temper of yours, and try to think before you open that delectable mouth in front of anyone else.'

His hand at her neck was sending shivers down her spine, and she stiffened involuntarily. 'I do not have a bad temper,' she flared.

He laughed and took her glass and put it down, then drew her into his arms. 'Whatever. Any uncontrolled outburst and this is how I will deal with it.'

His mouth covered hers, and he began an assault on her senses that left her meekly agreeing to his demands as he carried her up to bed.

Saffron squirmed restlessly on the towel and turned over on to her back. Even thinking about it now still had the power to make her blood run hotter in her veins. Last night Alex had made love to her with a slow, aching tenderness that had left her sensually replete but with a pain in her heart that had brought tears to her eyes. They had curled up to sleep in each other's arms like two halves of a whole, and oddly enough this morning Alex had delayed his departure for Athens until nine-thirty, long enough to bring her a cup of tea in bed and share breakfast with her.

Saffron did not understand the man at all. The villain she thought him to be did not equate with the Alex of this morning. He was a complete enigma to her, and she had a growing, disturbing conviction that she would never be free of the sexual hunger, her unrestrained longing for him.

It made no sense. For twenty-five years she had managed to retain a cool outward control over her temper and her body, but in no time at all Alex had turned her into a wild, sexy woman with a lightning-quick temper. It was almost unbelievable. Except that she loved him, a little voice inside her whispered, reminding her of what she was trying so hard to forget. She loved him...

The sound of a helicopter broke the silence, and she jumped to her feet, swiftly gathering up her things. She picked up her watch and slipped it on her wrist. Only four! She looked up and watched as the machine disappeared behind the house. Could it possibly be Alex back so early...? What was he playing at?

She walked across the sand to where the gate opened on to the first terrace and began the long climb back up to the house.

Alex met her on the lawn. 'I thought I'd join you for a swim; the heat in Athens is unbearable.'

He was stripped down to black swimming-trunks, a towel swung carelessly over one broad shoulder, his hard-muscled body gleaming golden in the sunlight, his eyes hidden from her by dark sunglasses.

'I've had a swim,' she said; she could not read his expression and it made her nervous.

'So indulge me, hmm?' And, catching her hand in his, he swept her around. 'I feel the need of some R and R, and preferably with you.' And once more Saffron descended to the beach with a heart that for some inexplicable reason suddenly felt much lighter.

They swam and frolicked in the clear blue water, and to Saffron's secret delight Alex made no effort to swim off for miles on his own as he usually did; instead they played a ridiculous game of tag and dunk, their mingled laughter and shouts of triumph at each tag echoing in the clear air, until they were both breathless and in Saffron's case almost half drowned.

Later, over a superb dinner served outside on the terrace, the house and garden aglow with hidden lights among the shrubs and trees, Saffron sighed as she drained her coffee-cup.

'Why the sigh, Saffron?' Alex queried softly.

'I was just thinking how perfect this setting is—the house, the lights, the weather—but . . .'

'But the company is not . . . Is that what you're trying to say?' he demanded hardly, the flash of anger in his dark eyes searing her to the bone.

'No, I was going to say, but I miss my work, that's all.' She did not want to spoil what had been a lovely day. She saw him visibly relax, and his dark eyes suddenly glinted with devilment.

'That's no problem.' Rising to his feet, he caught her hand and dragged Saffron to hers. 'Never let it be said that I deprive my wife of her work.' And, leading her into the house, he added, 'You can massage me any time.'

'I'd rather make you up,' she teased, not at all sure that she could massage Alex without jumping his bones.

'No way!' he exclaimed, horrified.

'Men should at the very least use a moisturiser. The old-fashioned colognes simply dry the masculine skin— no good at all,' Saffron blustered on, her pulse racing, and not with the effort of walking upstairs.

'Go bury yourself in the study, Alex. We ladies are going to have a hen party,' Anna instructed her son with the wave of a beringed hand.

Saffron could not repress a smile as she saw Alex's look of puzzlement and then his cautioning glance at herself, before he reluctantly walked off to his study. His mother, aunt and cousin had arrived for lunch, and over coffee it had been decided that Saffron would make all three of them up for tonight's dinner party. Anna had declared, 'What's the point of a beauty therapist in the family if we can't make use of her?' and Saffron had laughingly agreed.

In fact, as she carefully set out all her materials in Anna's bedroom, she could not help concluding that

Anna, far from being the poor, put-upon lady she had described when telling Saffron the sad story of her husband and Katherina, was in fact a very strong-willed woman. Look at the way the two older women had arrived together today, laughing and joking and obviously intent on enjoying their holiday. It didn't make sense.

But then nothing in her life for the past few months had made much sense. If she could only turn the clock back to May and the fateful day she had agreed to leave the agency and work solely for Anna Statis—safe and secure in London, no one to worry about but herself, no one to care about but herself—would she do it? Was that really what she wanted? To live out her life alone with only her work for company, never to have felt the touch of Alex's hands, the warmth of his embrace...? Saffron shuddered.

'Are you all right, Saffy, dear?'

Saffron swung round to face the door; only Anna ever called her Saffy. 'Yes, a ghost walked over my grave. It was nothing.' She could not let the older woman discover the truth about her marriage; Alex was her son and she loved him. Pinning a smile on her face, she asked, 'Right, who's first?'

For the next hour Saffron carefully applied her skills to making first Maria look stunning then Aunt Katherina and finally Anna. The conversation was pure woman talk—clothes, make-up and of course men...

Then Katherina began recounting a tale from when her first husband was alive.

'Remember, Anna, that time all of us were in London and you and Nikos were looking for a house to buy for Alex starting college? I had met my brother for lunch— he was living in London at the time—and afterwards I met up with you there again. Don't you remember? We were walking around Trafalgar Square.'

'Vaguely,' Anna replied.

'Well, my husband was so old-fashioned.' Katherina turned laughing brown eyes on Saffron. 'Rather like your Alex about family. Anyway, to get back to the story, when I told my husband my brother's new business venture was a partnership in a health club—Studio 96— he was furious, insisting the place was a massage parlour only one step removed from a brothel. We argued, and I chased him around Trafalgar Square, and finally I shoved him into the fountain.'

'Yes, I remember now.' Anna burst out laughing. 'You were screeching, "Anyway, how the hell do you know unless you've been there?"'

'That's right.' Katherina chuckled. 'He gave me some fairy-tale about a well-known aristocrat recommending the place. Then my poor husband died a few weeks later.'

'Saffy, that was my eye.' Anna's head moved to one side as Saffron's hand jerked with the mascara brush.

'What? Yes, sorry.' Saffron was shocked. How could these respectable old ladies be so casual about something so sordid? 'But weren't you horrified?' she could not help asking Katherina.

'Horrified, yes, but I didn't believe it.'

'Oh...' was all Saffron could muster, but her facial expression must have given her away because suddenly Katherina was very serious.

'Alex will probably kill me for telling you, but every family has its black sheep and unfortunately my brother Akis was ours; he believed in sailing close to the wind, but never anything out-and-out illegal. When he died seven years ago Alex had to go to London to arrange the transportation of his body to Greece for the funeral and sort out his business affairs. I doubt if he would have told me the truth, but I had seen the accounts for the health club—very profitable—and I could not see why it had to be sold. Finally Alex confessed the place was a very expensive massage parlour on the edge of the law.'

'It never belonged to Alex,' Saffron said hoarsely, the full enormity of what she had done finally sinking into her horrified mind.

The laughter of the other three sounded like the witches in *Macbeth* to Saffron's stunned brain.

'Good God, no!' Katherina exclaimed. 'Apparently he walked in one morning, cleared the place within half an hour, then signed over my brother's share to Akis's junior partner—an Italian, I think—for next to nothing simply to get rid of it before any, however tenuous, connection could get out and affect the Statis name and Alex's impeccable reputation. Goodness knows what went on there after that.'

'Cousin Alex, owning a massage parlour?' Maria hooted. 'The mind boggles! He is so strait-laced, he once stopped my allowance for a month simply because at eighteen I shared a holiday apartment in Paris with another girl and a *boy*!'

Saffron tried to smile, to join in the obvious amusement of the other three, as she finally, with a none too steady hand put the finishing touches to Anna's make-up. Then she quickly gathered up her kit and, with a deep-felt sigh of relief, made her excuses and left Anna's room to return to the comparative safety of the master bedroom.

She dropped her make-up case on the bed and, like an automaton, slipped off her simple cotton skirt and blouse. On leaden feet she walked into the bathroom, stepped out of her briefs and unfastened her bra, letting it fall to the marble floor. She walked into the huge double shower and turned on the overhead spray, her mind in chaos. Lifting her face to the warm water, she let it wash over her, wishing it would wash her mind clear as easily.

How could she have been so dumb? He own common sense should have told her that Alex, with all his wealth, would not be bothered about a part-share in some seedy massage parlour.

'My God, what have I done?' she cried, unaware that she had said the words out loud.

The folding glass door was pushed open and a naked Alex joined her. 'What have you done?' he queried mockingly, his hands reaching out for her shoulders, holding her steady. 'Let me guess—slipped and shaved their eyebrows off.' He raised his dark brows teasingly. 'Or hopefully glued their mouths shut?' he prompted with a wry grin.

Saffron, her green eyes wide on his roughly handsome face, was suddenly struck by the realisation of how little she knew her husband. They were as intimate as it was possible for two people to be in the physical sense, and yet on a mental level she had never even tried to find out what made him tick. She had clung to her own opinion and prejudice unquestioningly. It had not occurred to her to try and delve beneath the macho, arrogant mask he presented to the world, even to consider that there might be a more sensitive soul beneath.

Her gaze slid lovingly over his broad shoulders, the massive hairy chest, his slim waist, narrow hips and long, long legs. The water cascaded over his bronzed flesh like a lover's caress, flowing over hard-packed muscle and sinew. She reached up her hand and gently outlined his firm mouth, down his chin, then trailed her fingers down into the damp forest of hair surrounding the small male nipple. He was her husband, and she . . . she had . . . She could not bear to think of what a fool she had been . . .

'Saffron,' Alex murmured huskily. But even as her touch aroused him, 'What is it?' he asked, recognising the change in her.

Trust, that was what she had lacked; she should have trusted him. And yet it was not entirely her fault—her upbringing had taught her to trust no one. In that second she took a great leap of faith, and, tilting back her head, looked straight up into his concerned dark eyes.

'You never owned Studio 96; that day I saw you there was the first and only time you'd been there, wasn't it?'

Alex stiffened, his fingers tightening on her shoulders, his expression suddenly bland. 'So?'

'Why did you let me believe it was yours? Why? Why did you not tell me the truth, deny my accusation?'

'Why should I? It changes nothing.'

'But it does, don't you see?' Saffron was getting desperate. 'If I had known I would never have even contemplated revenge. I would never have told you about Eve. We would have married and everything would have been fine.' How could he not understand? Her puzzled eyes searched his face.

'Everything *is* fine, my sweet Saffron,' he drawled softly, pulling her closer to him; her naked breasts snuggled into his damp body hair and hard flesh as his strong hands stroked down her back and curved over her bottom, hauling her against the taut heat of his arousal. 'Couldn't be better,' he husked against her mouth as his lips found hers.

'Wait, Alex,' Saffron murmured a long moment later. 'I want to explain.' It seemed imperative to her that she confess her foolishness in believing Alex capable of such despicable behaviour. She would get on her knees and beg his forgiveness if she had to.

He held her away from him, his darkening eyes raking her from head to toe in a long, lingering scrutiny. The water had plastered her wild curls flat to her head, the rest straggling like rats' tails down her back. She had no idea of how desirable she looked, her small face flushed, her gorgeous green eyes pleading, her full breasts hard-tipped, pouting, and his gaze moved lower to the tiny waist, the soft flare of her feminine hips, and smooth, shapely legs. 'There is nothing to explain, Saffron,' Alex declared throatily.

'But there is,' she wailed, amazed at his denseness. 'Katherina told me all about her brother—the black sheep of the family—and the health club. If only...'

'"If only..." Really, Saffron, have we come to that—the tritest phrase in the English language?' With a snort of disgust, he stepped out of the shower stall and, collecting two towels, threw one to her. His expression grim, he hitched the other towel strategically around his hips.

'You want to talk? OK, we'll talk. Dry yourself; if I touch you again, conversation will definitely be out.' And, turning, he strode out of the bathroom.

Saffron rubbed herself dry, swiftly wrapped the fluffy towel under her arms and over her breasts sarong style, and dashed after him.

He was sitting on the edge of the bed and his dark, assessing eyes lifted to her flushed face. She walked towards him and stopped a foot away; it was strange to be looking down on Alex for a change, and somehow it gave her confidence to ask, 'Why did you not tell me on our wedding night when I accused you of...? Well, you know what.'

'Because, Saffron, I did not think it that important. I know who and what I am; the misguided opinions of other people hold no interest for me.'

'But we were married.'

'Yes, but a marriage licence did not give me licence to blacken my aunt Katherina's name.'

Saffron had never felt so small in her life; while she had ranted about Eve, her dead friend, Alex, however misguided his reasons, had remained silent to protect a female member of his family. For once, her mind clear of the guilt and chaotic emotions that had beleaguered her from first meeting Alex, she saw the man beneath the hard, sophisticated surface. How could she have been so blind? Alex was half Greek and all male; it was an integral part of his nature to protect the family, especially the female members.

She stepped forward between his knees and, reaching down, placed her hands either side of his head, her fingers tangling in the damp black hair. Tilting back his head, she bent and, for the first time in their relationship, kissed him full on his sensual lips. She put her heart and soul into it, and when she finally lifted her head Alex's hands were firmly clasped around her thighs.

'What was that for?' His eyes, holding a gleam of amusement, slanted upwards. 'Not that I'm complaining,' he drawled, and fell back on the bed, taking Saffron with him.

'Because I love you, you fool.' Saffron laughed out loud; her legs trapped between his powerful thighs, she lay sprawled across his broad chest. 'And you're too damn macho, too noble for your own good,' she teased, biting lightly down on a very tempting male nipple.

'Noble, eh?' Alex repeated with obvious pleasure. 'A vast improvement on being a crook, pimp et cetera. Noble I can live with.' And, in a lightning move, Saffron was flat on her back, her feet on the floor, and Alex was between her thighs, leaning over her.

Her slender arms looped around his neck, her heart full of love and laughter. She felt light-headed with joy. The sense of betrayal she had felt towards Eve at the pleasure she found in Alex's arms no longer existed. The man indirectly responsible for Eve's death had nothing to do with her husband. She was free, free, free . . .

Pulling his head down until his mouth was a breath away from hers, she whispered, 'And I can live with you, my noble Alex, my love . . .'

He looked at her for a moment, his face grave, questioning, as if he doubted her words. Then his mouth came down on hers, crushing her lips against her teeth in a sudden savage assault. She opened her mouth, welcoming his passion as her body arched up to him, urging the more powerful, steely invasion of his masculine form.

There was no need for preliminaries; her body was hot and waiting for him. His large hands slid down around her waist and hauled her on to him and she clung to him, buffeted by wave after wave of passion, until a tumultuous release shook her to the depths of her soul and Alex, with a shuddering cry, spilled his life force into her. For a moment his hands tightened around her waist and his lips brushed hers in a tender kiss.

Then abruptly he straightened up. 'That was not so noble of me,' he said at last, his voice low, his dark eyes intense.

Saffron smiled up at him. 'I enjoyed it; I always enjoy you,' she confessed freely, happily.

Their eyes met and clung, and then Alex's lips quirked in the beginnings of a smile. 'My spicy Saffron,' he drawled endearingly, 'I'm beginning to think I will never get enough of you as long as I live, but right now three beautifully made-up women are waiting downstairs to greet the rest of our guests—the yacht is due to dock any minute with about a dozen friends and business associates.'

'A dozen more . . .' She gasped her dismay.

'Not to worry, Saffron. Despina has it all under control.'

She felt a brief twinge of resentment. Obviously Alex had not thought her capable of arranging a large party, and that hurt. Did he still see her as simply a plaything? Surely not after the afternoon they had just spent together?

'Come on, we will share the shower.' He held out his hand and she trustingly took it and allowed him to pull her to her feet. 'But this time let's try and get washed, hmm?'

Half an hour later Saffron walked down the stairs on Alex's arm, her earlier doubts forgotten. She felt as though she was floating on air. Alex was magnificent in a white dinner-jacket and she knew she looked good too. She had swept her red hair up in a bunch of curls on her crown, leaving a few stray curls to hang tantalisingly on her bare shoulders. Her dress was a strapless cream wisp of silk that contrasted beautifully with her golden skin. The skirt was straight, ending just above her knees, revealing her long, tanned legs, and on her feet she wore high-heeled gold sandals. Around her slender throat hung a brilliant diamond and emerald necklace—a gift from Alex only five minutes earlier.

It was the best party Saffron had ever attended, though, as the hostess, she knew it was conceited of her to think so. Sixteen sat down at the elegant dining-table for the formal meal. The food was superb, the conversation scintillating, and everyone appeared to be having a marvellous time. Alex was at the head of the table and Saffron at the opposite end, but it did not seem to matter; she felt closer to him tonight than ever before. Occasionally their eyes would meet and a swift secret smile pass between them. He gave her confidence with just a glance.

Luckily she had Katherina and Spiros, Maria and James nearest to her, so it was not as if she was among total strangers. The rest of the guests were fashionable and wealthy and regarded Saffron with avid interest, trying to decide just what there was about her that had captured the mighty Alex. She could not suppress a smile at some of the more blatant questions, but with Alex's help managed to field them expertly.

Coffee was served out on the terrace, and the party became informal. Soft music played from strategically placed speakers and a few people elected to dance, but most settled into comfortable groups, chatting about friends and relatives, and, as with most Greek parties, the alcohol flowed as freely as the conversation.

Saffron stepped back out of the circle of light and leant against the balustrade, surveying the laughing faces of her guests—a moment's breather, she thought. Then James approached her.

'Congratulations, Saffron, on your marriage and on your first house party. You're a natural.'

'House party?' she queried. 'Dinner party surely?'

'No, Saffron, most of us are staying on the yacht, the rest here, for the next two days. Surely Alex told you?'

'Yes—yes, of course.' But he hadn't! Though she refused to let James see her embarrassment, was it pity she saw in his pale eyes?

'Don't worry, I'm a push-over for a beautiful lady. If you need any help, give me a call.'

'That's highly unlikely,' she said with a slightly forced smile. 'But thanks for the offer.'

'James, Maria needs a drink; see to it.' Alex's curt command put an end to what for Saffron was a disturbing conversation. 'OK, Saffron?' he queried, reaching her side and putting a possessive arm around her waist.

She shot him an angry glance. 'Yes, of course. Why? Were you worried that I would be incapable of looking after your friends for *two* days? Frightened I might disgrace you?' she snapped, James's words lingering in her mind.

Alex muttered a curse under his breath and in full view of everyone turned her in his arms, his hard mouth hovering inches from hers. 'Foolish girl, you're far too sensitive, and for what it's worth I don't think you could disgrace yourself if you tried. You're too much a lady— my very lovely lady.'

Their breath met and mingled, and his lips, firm and tender, moved against hers. Saffron vaguely heard the cheers of encouragement, and not so proper comments, but, locked in his arms, she forgot her anger and her doubt; she knew no shame, no embarrassment, only a deep, abiding love for the man who held her so close to his heart.

CHAPTER NINE

Two days later Anna and Saffron stood in the garden and watched the yacht carrying the guests depart for Athens.

'That was without a doubt the best house party ever, Saffy, dear,' Anna remarked complacently. 'You're a natural when it comes to putting people at their ease. Maybe it has something to do with your training. But I want you to know I couldn't have wished for a better daughter-in-law. You make Alex the perfect wife and it was obvious to everyone he loves you dearly.'

'That was your son's fault.' Saffron raised one finely arched eyebrow at Anna. 'He saw me talking to James and decided to take action.'

Anna laughed. 'Yes, a good dose of jealousy was just what my arrogant son needed to appreciate you fully. I've watched him and he has never been more than an arm's length away all weekend.'

A secret smile curved Saffron's lips. And at night he had been a whole lot closer, she thought dreamily. It was going to work; her marriage was going to be a great success, and she was slowly beginning to believe that there was such a thing as happy ever after.

Life took on a new zest. Anna was a marvellous companion, and a great raconteuse, and as October and most of November slipped by Saffron had never been so happy. The discovery that Alex had never intended to keep her a prisoner on the island only added to her respect for him. The first week of her mother-in-law's visit

Saffron had been stunned when Anna had said one morning, 'Come on, let's go to Athens.'

When Saffron had said there was no transport, Anna had laughed out loud. Apparently, the male bar Saffron had not dared enter was also the local ferry. She could have walked in any time and asked the proprietor, and his son would have taken her to the mainland in his speedboat for one thousand drachma—next to nothing!

'Well, what do you think?' Saffron walked the length of the bedroom and back, an exaggerated sway to her slim hips. 'Your mother loved it.'

She had been shopping in Athens with Anna; the older woman was leaving for England the next day and had insisted on one last shopping trip, then had quite shamelessly encouraged Saffron to use her husband's credit card like a woman with ten hands, saying that Saffy needed a winter wardrobe.

With dinner over, and in the privacy of their own bedroom, she was putting on a fashion show for Alex. Fresh from the shower, he lay sprawled on the bed, a towel covering the essentials, his dark eyes following her around the room.

She glanced back over her shoulder at him. 'So...?' she prompted, slowly turning and running her hands lightly over her hips, smoothing the already figure-hugging fabric of the electric-blue jumpsuit even tighter to her body. She watched Alex's eyes darken as he followed the trail of her hands, and then lazily he allowed his glance to meander up her body, stopping at the proud thrust of her breasts, the nipples clearly outlined by the clinging wool jersey, the deep cleavage where she had left the zip only partly fastened. She was tempting him and loving it . . .

'So, my sweet, sexy wife,' he drawled finally, raising his gaze to hers. 'Two questions. Do you expect me to take you skiing? And as a man I'm no expert on these all-in-one things, but isn't it an effort to go to the lavatory?'

'Oh, Alex, how prosaic,' she groaned. 'Here I am trying to seduce you and you come out with a question like that.'

'I hate to disillusion you, Saffron, but most men prefer to be seduced by women in floaty bits of silk and lace underwear, not a wool suit reminiscent of a battle dress that will take some time to remove.'

'We could put it to the test,' she murmured throatily, approaching the bed and lowering the zip still further. Alex looked so good lying there, tanned and relaxed, and it had been almost twenty-four hours since the last time they had made love.

'Is this a none too subtle way of getting out of telling me how much money you've spent today?' Alex queried cynically, his dark eyes mocking her. 'Because if it is it is quite unnecessary. As I've told you before, I have money enough to last a hundred lifetimes; you don't have to pay for each item you buy with sex.'

Saffron stopped; she felt as if she had been punched in the stomach. Her green eyes sought Alex's; he had pulled himself up and was sitting propped up on the bed, the pillow at his back, and his expression was one of cool disdain. Was that what he truly thought?

All the colour drained from her face and she stared at him, unable to believe that he had said that, and some tiny devil inside her whispered, Is he right? Did I set out to seduce him tonight because of all the money I've spent? No! her heart cried in denial. It was not like that. She loved Alex with every fibre of her being.

She stepped forward, and stopped again. But all these weeks when she had thought they were making love Alex had never mentioned *love*. Did he see it as just sex?

'The thought never entered my head,' she managed to say lightly, but it was beyond her capabilities to carry on with the seduction she had planned. 'So you don't like the blue. I must remember that,' she murmured, pulling the zip right up to the neck before turning away from his lounging figure, adding, 'I'll show you the rest some other time. I need a shower.' And she escaped into the bathroom.

Two hours later she was lying in the big bed, the sound of Alex's even breathing the only noise in the quiet room, but sleep was elusive. In her euphoria at realising that Alex was not the swine she had thought, she had rashly declared her love, and somehow assumed he felt the same, but his words this evening had burst her bright balloon of happiness.

She turned over restlessly and slid her arm around his waist to hug him. They had made love, and it had been as good as always—she was worrying unnecessarily, she tried to tell herself, but sleep when it finally came was shallow and broken.

In the morning Anna departed with Alex for Athens and Saffron was once again virtually alone and very aware of the isolation of her island home. She told herself she would soon settle down, but when Alex called a couple of hours later and told her he would not be home that night—a vital meeting—doubts about herself and him plagued her mind.

Was she really cut out for the life of a lady of leisure, waiting on a paradise island until her husband needed her, her dream of her own beauty salon just that—a dream? Strangely restless, she strolled along the beach.

The summer had gone and a cold wind blew in off the sea. In a few more weeks it would be Christmas.

Then it came to her. Why stay on the island? Alex commuted to Athens, so why couldn't she? Perhaps she could open a salon, or work in a city hospital as a clinical beautician; there were dozens of opportunities if she really sought them.

Fired up with enthusiasm and eager to discuss the idea with Alex, she returned to the house, packed an overnight bag and called the local bar to book the ferry for the mainland. She would surprise Alex, cook him dinner in his small *pied-à-terre* in Athens, and maybe tomorrow look for suitable premises. Always supposing Alex was agreeable... And always supposing he loved her... the voice of reality rang in her mind. But she refused to listen; she didn't dare because she was almost certain she had already fulfilled one part of their bargain: she needed to buy a pregnancy-test kit. But she could be a mother *and* a businesswoman!

Saffron walked into the glass and steel structure that was Alex's corporate headquarters, and went straight to the directors' lift. She walked out at the top floor and into the reception area. She had visited the office a couple of times with Alex and the secretary recognised her.

'Mrs Statis. This is a surprise. I'm not sure your husband is here.'

'It's not that important; I only wanted to collect the spare key for his apartment—I know he leaves one here.'

The young girl opened the top door of her desk and handed over the key. 'Well, you are his wife so it must be all right,' she said with a smile.

At that moment a door opened at the rear of the office and James strolled out. He stopped, his blond head going back as he saw Saffron. Did he hesitate before dashing across to take her hand, or was it her imagination?

'Saffron, lovely to see you, but what brings you here? I don't think Alex is expecting you.'

'No, I want to surprise him; I've had a great idea and I can't wait to tell him.'

'Well, he isn't here.'

'No, that's a shame; still, he did say he was busy and was going to be working late, but when he gets in touch can you tell him I'll be waiting at the apartment?'

'Apartment! Do you think that's a good idea?' James questioned, his blue eyes oddly intent on her smiling face. 'Why not allow me to take you for an early dinner and arrange for the helicopter to fly you home? I'm sure Alex really will be very late.'

Saffron's eager optimism was trickling away. Perhaps she had been a bit rash, but still it could do no harm to wait for Alex, even if it was midnight when he got back. 'No, James, really; it's nice of you to offer, but I'll be perfectly all right on my own until Alex arrives.'

'But I'm not sure I can get in touch with him. It is a very important meeting,' James responded with a strange urgency, and was it sympathy she saw in his blue eyes? Surely not...

'Look, James, don't worry,' she said over-brightly. 'I'm going to hit the shops for an hour or two. I'll be fine.'

'Here, take my card; if you need...' He stumbled over the words, most unlike his usual suave, very English self. 'If you change your mind call me at home.'

'Yes, OK.' She took the card from his outstretched hand and beat a hasty retreat. Somehow James's attitude worried her, and why, as Alex's PA, wasn't he with him, if it was such a vital meeting?

*   *   *

The apartment was small, with a kitchen, living-room, bathroom, bedroom and balcony. Saffron had visited it with Alex when she had been in Athens, but only for a few minutes while he dropped off his briefcase. He had told her that Athens, although home of the Acropolis and some of the most marvellous ancient ruins in the world, was also the second most polluted city in the world. The traffic was horrendous and the smell of carbon monoxide hung in the air twenty-four hours a day. No one made it their permanent home if they could avoid it. She'd forgotten that in her rush to make plans, but it wasn't important, she told herself firmly.

With her shopping lying on the floor, a cup of coffee in front of her, Saffron settled on the sofa and, curling her feet up beneath her, felt quite at home. She heard a key turn in the lock and turned her head towards the door, a broad smile lighting her lovely face. Alex was back, and not that late after all. But when the door opened her smile vanished and her eyes widened in shock as Sylvia walked in as if she owned the place.

'Well, a visitor. What are you doing here?' the dark-headed woman asked casually, dumping a briefcase on the table in front of Saffron.

'I could ask you the same question,' Saffron shot back. She had not seen the other woman since the wedding, and she had deliberately refused to think about Sylvia's relationship with Alex, convincing herself that it was all in the past—another ostrich act, some simple explanation for Sylvia's being here, having a key... Perhaps she was delivering something for Alex. Yes, that must be it.

'I live here.'

Saffron stared, struck dumb. Sylvia lived here... in Alex's apartment. It wasn't possible. Slowly she uncurled herself and stood up; she was not going to let this woman intimidate her. She was Alex's wife.

'I don't believe you.'

The other woman, her dark eyes glittering malevolently, said, 'Follow me, if you dare,' and headed towards the bedroom door.

On trembling legs Saffron followed her, and watched as she slid back a mirrored wardrobe door to reveal a row of feminine clothes, and then quite deliberately slid back the next door, revealing more clothes, but this time Saffron could not fail to recognise a couple of masculine suits, shoes and shirts. Alex's!

'You're a fool, Saffron; you didn't really think Alex was the type to settle for one woman, did you? He only married you to please his mother. I did warn you on the yacht—you should have listened.'

'Yes—yes, I should...' Saffron whispered, and, turning on her heel, she walked back to the living-room. Her gaze grazed over the shopping she had left on the floor; the name of a pharmacy on one package brought a bitter twist to her lips. Now was not the time to discover if she was pregnant.

Picking up the parcels and her jacket, she walked out into the cold, dark night. Some time later a screech of brakes shocked her back to reality and prevented her being mown down by a huge truck.

She jumped back on the pavement and stared about her. She had no idea where she was or how far she had walked. The rain was beating down, a storm brewing, and her skirt and blouse were soaked. She put her hand in her jacket pocket, her fingers curling around the card James had given her earlier. Now his offer of assistance, the sympathy she had seen in his eyes made sense. As Alex's PA James must have known about Sylvia all along; probably all Alex's business acquaintances did—

the people at the house party! Tears blurred her vision; her shame and humiliation were complete.

The little wife, his mother's choice, tucked away on the island, living in cloud-cuckoo land, imagining herself loved. What a naïve fool she had been, and she had only herself to blame.

But no more, she vowed silently, brushing the tears from her eyes. Straightening her shoulders, she glanced once again at the card in her hand. Why not? she thought. At least James could help her get back to England.

'Saffron!' James exclaimed, taking in at a glance the distraught state of the woman at his door. 'Come in. You're drenched; what happened?'

Saffron forced a brief attempt at a smile, but her lips quivered, her eyes filling with tears, and she gave up trying. 'Nothing much, James,' she said sadly. 'Nothing that can't be cured with a ticket to England on the first available flight. That's why I'm here; could you fix it for me, please?' And, walking past him, she collapsed on the first seat she reached in his comfortable living-room.

James, bless him, did not ask questions; he simply poured her a large brandy, watched while she drank it, and then directed her to the bathroom, handing her his bathrobe and instructing her to get out of her wet clothes; they could talk later. Saffron was glad of his restraint; she had the horrible conviction that if she once began talking about her marriage she would fall apart completely and irreversibly.

She had to concentrate single-mindedly on getting back to England. Standing naked under the warm spray of the shower, she chanted under her breath, 'Flight, hotel, work,' over and over again. She had been alone most of her life, except for Eve! The tears threatened again, but she clenched her teeth and refused to give in to them. Eve's last message, urging her not to let any man get to her, but to pursue her dream of starting her own business, whirled around in her mind.

She had been side-tracked from her ambition, but not any more. On the island of Mykonos she had fallen in love, flustered and flattered when Alex had likened her to a Rossini overture, but now his softly murmured comment at the time, which she had conveniently ignored, came back to haunt her. He had said that he hoped the title did not accurately reflect her as well: *The Thieving Magpie*.

He had never seen her as anything other than a greedy woman in cahoots with his mother to trap him into marriage. He had gone along with the plan because it suited him to do so. He lusted after her body. Nothing more. In fairness to him, she was forced to admit that he had never pretended it was anything else. She had fooled herself. In love for the first time in her life, and with the matter of Alex's involvement with the health club resolved, she had naïvely assumed that because she loved Alex he must love her. Talk about rose-coloured spectacles...

The last few months were a nightmare she had to forget, pretend had never happened. Deep in her inner being she had known from the start that her relationship with Alex was doomed to failure. Eve apart, she quite simply was not in Alex's sophisticated league and did not really want to be. She had been a fool to believe otherwise. The pain in her chest would fade. Hearts did not break, she told herself firmly, ignoring the ache in her own; they simply atrophied.

She stepped out of the shower, turned off the water and picked up a couple of towels from the rail. She wrapped one around her wet hair and rubbed herself dry with the other until her soft skin was red with the effort, then pulled on the robe James had given her, grimacing wryly at the colour. Black! How fitting! she thought bitterly. The death of love! The death of a marriage! The death of foolish dreams!

She must stop thinking like that, she remonstrated with herself, and, moving to the vanity basin with the mirror and wall-mounted hairdrier above, she unwrapped the towel from her head. For a second she thought she heard a ringing in her ears; probably lack of food, she told herself staunchly, and, turning on the drier, began to run her fingers methodically through her long red locks. She didn't see her reflection in the mirror; she didn't want to; instead she succumbed to the mindless task of drying her hair, oddly soothing to her shattered emotions.

Finally, her toilet complete, she stared at her reflection, sure that the traumatic events of the evening must have marked her for life. But she saw the same ginger-headed, solitary girl she had always been. Reassured, she turned to leave the room, and only someone who knew her well could have recognised the change... The green eyes, once sparkling with life, quick to flash in humour or anger, were oddly opaque; the light had died from them, and with it an intrinsic part of Saffron was lost...

She tightened the belt around her waist, rolled the overlong sleeves of the robe halfway up her arms and silently, barefoot, moved down the short corridor. She pushed open the door of the living-room. Time to face James, get his help and get on with her life...

James was sitting on a wing-chair; his blond head turned as she entered, his blue eyes flashing a negative message she didn't understand.

Slowly her gaze slid to the opposite side of the fireplace and a long sofa. Alex! Alex was here, his black hair damp and plastered to his broad brow, his dark eyes narrowed to mere slits in the bronzed sculpture of his face, his sensuous mouth a thin slash of barely controlled fury. For a second, in the tense silence, Saffron thought she heard his teeth grinding together.

His piercing eyes raked her from head to toe, taking in the wild, freshly washed hair, the low V of the man's robe skimming her breasts, the cinched waist and the bare feet. His gaze returned to her face, and the implacable rage, the contempt glittering in his eyes would have intimidated her at any other time, but not tonight. Tonight her heart had died; she was numb, her emotions buried, as frozen as an Arctic ice-cap.

Silently Alex rose to his feet, his large hands curled into fists at his side. Idly Saffron noted that his knuckles gleamed white, and watched as his proud head turned to pin James with a lethal look.

'So this was why you told me you hadn't time to discuss the new business, James. You were entertaining my wife.'

'Entertaining, no. Saffron came for my help, nothing more.'

'And I can see what kind of help you gave her. The bitch is standing there naked beneath your robe.' Alex's hand gestured wildly to where Saffron was standing immobile as he lunged forward, towering over James. 'Stand up, you bastard, so I can knock you flat,' he roared like an enraged lion.

Saffron cried out, 'No—no, you're wrong,' shocked by the murderous look on Alex's face.

Ignoring her, Alex grabbed James by his shirt-front and hauled him to his feet; his fist shot out and knocked

James straight back into the chair with a crunching blow to his face.

'Stop it! Stop it!' Saffron dashed across the room and grabbed Alex's raised fist as he prepared to repeat his action.

'Listen to your wife,' James drawled with remarkable English restraint considering his nose was pouring blood. 'One punch I'll take—the situation could be misconstrued, I'll grant you. But two and I'll retaliate,' he offered phlegmatically.

'Please, Alex,' Saffron pleaded, hanging on to his arm. 'Leave James alone.' He shook her off as he would dispense with a fly and she fell heavily to the floor, a cry of shocked pain escaping her.

Alex turned his furious gaze on her dishevelled form; her robe had fallen open to reveal a long, shapely leg. 'You conniving, enticing bitch, I should kill you,' he snarled.

For a second the breath was knocked out of her, and she gazed helplessly up at him, convinced that he would carry out his threat. It was in his voice and the wild, primitive savagery in his black eyes.

He looked at her for a long, tense moment, then, like a mask falling, his expression changed; his dark eyes went blank and only a small muscle jerking beneath the skin of his cheek revealed his inner turmoil as he added scathingly, 'But you're not worth swinging for.' With a last contemptuous glance at her sprawled body, he spun back to James. 'As for you, clear your desk tomorrow; I never want to see you again.' Then, turning to where Saffron had struggled to her feet, he snarled, 'Get dressed; we're leaving.'

She did not argue, simply stalked past him to the bathroom and hauled her damp clothes back on. Head high, she marched back into the room, and before she had a chance to open her mouth she was swung over Alex's shoulder in a fireman's lift. But by the time she realised what had happened he was out of the door and marching towards the car.

'Put me down!' she screamed, her temper flaring white-hot; she thumped his broad back with her curled fists, but it was like trying to dent steel.

'Shut up, just shut up,' Alex growled, flinging her into the front seat of the car and slamming the door. She made to get out again, but he was too fast; in seconds he was in the driving seat and hurtling the car through the city traffic like a man possessed.

She fastened her seatbelt then glanced at him with cold, furious eyes. How dared he suggest for one minute that she and James...? Deceitful, debauched son of Satan! she cursed silently. 'Bloody Neanderthal brute,' she swore out loud. She shot forward as the car screeched to a halt, only her seatbelt saving her from hitting the windscreen.

Alex's hard hand caught her chin and turned her face towards his. 'Don't you ever swear at me again. I won't tolerate any more from you,' he grated, his hand on her face shaking with the force of his rage.

'That's rich coming from you,' she shot back. 'At least my meeting with James was perfectly innocent.' Not like his permanent arrangement with Sylvia, and as she remembered her reason for going to James in the first place the anger that had consumed her for the past half-hour vanished. What was the point?

'*Innocent*?' he sneered with cynical disbelief. 'Wearing only the man's robe? What do you take me for—an idiot...?'

She opened her mouth to respond, but Alex locked the words in her throat as he covered her mouth with his own; his fingers dug into the flesh of her jaw while his mouth ground against hers in a raging travesty of a kiss, forcing her lips against her teeth, stealing the breath from her body until she thought she would choke.

For once her body did not respond in its usual wanton way. She felt nothing but horror and disgust as his other hand closed over the damp material of her blouse and roughly kneaded her breast until finally, as he sensed her lack of response, with a muffled curse, his hands dropped from her face and breast and she fell back against the seat, gasping for breath, her green eyes stormy with suppressed fury.

'Sated by James... But not for long. I know your wanton ways too well,' he opined with sneering sarcasm, and, swinging back to the steering-wheel, he started the car again.

Saffron curbed the angry impulse that made her want to scream her hurt and rage at his hateful face; instead she closed her eyes, blocking him from her view as she blocked him from her heart. Where he was taking her she didn't know and didn't much care. The marriage was over; he could keep his Sylvia and good luck to them. The side of himself Alex had displayed tonight had horrified her and only confirmed what she had already decided, what she had always known... She was better off on her own...

CHAPTER TEN

TEN minutes later Saffron was strapped into the helicopter and Alex was at the controls. The rain lashed the reinforced glass and the wind buffeted the fragile fuselage. 'Isn't it rather stormy for flying?' she asked icily, pulling her soaking clothes around her shivering flesh.

'If we go, we go together. Till death us do part and all that—something you have obviously forgotten,' Alex responded with mocking cynicism.

Saffron shot him a furious glance and pressed her lips together. Let him play his two-faced game, she thought. She knew he had kept Sylvia as his mistress, and to try and tar her—Saffron—with the same brush was simply despicable and not worth denying.

She felt some sympathy for James. He did not deserve to lose his job because of her, and on the short, stormy flight to Serendipidos she resolved that when she had finally left the island for good, which she fully intended doing at the first opportunity, a letter exonerating James must be one of her first priorities.

By the time she was standing once more in the reception hall of the villa, Saffron was frozen to the bone and shivering from head to foot.

'For God's sake, woman, do you want to get pneumonia?' Alex exclaimed, and, picking her up yet again, he carried her upstairs and into the bathroom. Ruthlessly he stripped her naked, his face like thunder as he turned on the shower tap and pushed her beneath the hot, reviving jets. 'Can you manage or shall I help?'

She tossed her head back, her green eyes burning with bitter resentment. 'No way,' she snapped back, but her chattering teeth rather spoiled her defiant attitude.

Alex stared at her naked, shivering form for a tense, angry moment, then spun on his heel and strode out of the bathroom, the violent crashing of the door making even the shower spray quiver.

The next day, Saffron awoke from a deep sleep to the sound of the helicopter departing. She stretched out a hand to where Alex had lain, as she did every morning, seeking the security and comfort of his lingering warmth, when it hit her! It was finished, over. She hauled herself up into a sitting position and glanced across the wide bed to the other pillow; it was smooth, unused.

She should be grateful, she told herself; at least Alex had had the decency to sleep somewhere else last night. After her shower, exhausted by the day's events, she had crawled into bed, her body warm, her heart a frozen lump in her chest.

A cross between a yawn and a sigh escaped her as, swinging her feet to the floor, she slipped out of bed and moved to the window. The sky was a uniform grey; it fitted her mood exactly. She glanced down at the garden; the ravages of the storm were very evident— broken branches scattered the lawn and the flowers still blooming in November were now flattened to the earth. A bit like herself, she thought sadly.

She glanced at the sea; it was cold and black, but calm. She could leave today; there was nothing to keep her here any more. Alex had never cared for her. Oh, he had raved when he'd found her with James, but it had not been out of jealousy or any real emotion. It had simply been a male reaction to an apparent blow to his ego.

Saffron turned and walked across to the dressing-room, the set of her shoulders taut and somehow lonely. Slowly she packed her case with her own clothes, barely glancing at the things Alex had bought her, pushing them to one side without a thought. She felt nothing. Zombie-like, she washed and dressed in blue jeans and a wool shirt—ideal for travelling. She carried her case and holdall into the bedroom, placed her navy reefer jacket over the top, and then picked up the telephone.

She rang the airport, and within minutes was booked on a flight from Athens to London leaving that afternoon. She glanced at her wristwatch; it was nine-thirty, so she had plenty of time.

Despina gave her a funny look as she walked down the stairs carrying her bags. 'You go?' she said in frac-tured English.

Saffron simply smiled, a twist of her lips that did not reach her eyes, and strode into the kitchen. She helped herself to coffee and sipped it slowly, staring blankly out of the window. Her stomach rumbled loudly. I must eat something, she thought, trying to remember the last time she had eaten. Yesterday morning.

She eyed the loaf of bread that had been left on the table, strode over and cut off a chunk. She chewed the tasteless fare, her small face pale, her green eyes remote as she did so.

Five minutes later she walked out of the house with her belongings and never looked back.

The bar was almost empty, except for the proprietor. Saffron calmly requested a ride to the mainland. He gave her a puzzled look, but instructed his son to get the boat ready.

With a soft, 'Thank you,' Saffron sat down on a hardwood chair at a precariously balanced plastic table. She stacked her bags next to each other and then checked

her purse. She had money and her passport; everything
was in order. Soon, very soon, it would all be over...

The bar door swung open; the boat had arrived. She
half rose, glancing sideways at the open door, and sank
back down on the seat as Alex walked in.

His dark gaze flicked over her still form, and on down
to where her cases stood. 'Going somewhere?' he asked
flatly.

'I didn't hear the helicopter,' she murmured, her eyes
going to his hard face. He looked dreadful—unshaven,
his eyes sunken in their sockets, his mouth a grim narrow
line, like a man who had not slept for a week.

Alex stared at her. 'I came across on the yacht.'

'The yacht?' she parroted, unable to think clearly. She
had her departure planned, and it did not include seeing
Alex again.

Alex stepped closer and stopped, thrusting his hands
into the pockets of his faded jeans, pulling the fabric
taut across his muscular thighs.

Saffron's eyes followed his actions and incredibly her
frozen heart jerked painfully inside her. 'I'm just
leaving,' she said quickly.

'Yes, I know.' Alex moved and, bending, picked up
her case and bag. 'Let me help you.' And before she
could object he was striding out of the door.

She leapt to her feet and dashed after him. 'No, wait.
I can manage...' Her voice petered out as she saw the
yacht moored alongside the jetty and Alex standing on
the gangway leading to the *Lion Lore*.

He turned; his burning dark eyes raked over her. 'I
can't,' he said in a gruff voice. 'Get on board or I'll
carry you.'

She closed her eyes briefly. This cannot be happening,
she told herself, but when she opened them again Alex
was still waiting. She glanced at the silent men standing

around. Obviously they had been awaiting the arrival of the yacht to assist in the mooring. She had never looked out to sea. What an idiot! There was a long, intense silence; only the lapping of the water against the jetty broke the quiet. It was as if everyone was watching to see what would happen next.

'Saffron...' Alex's voice cracked like a whip.

She looked at him. 'A lift to the mainland,' she prompted, in an attempt to preserve some pride, and forced herself to move. She flinched as he placed a large hand under her elbow and urged her on board. He glanced at her and withdrew the hand as soon as they reached the deck.

'Go below; there isn't a full crew and another storm is brewing. I have to help.'

Her arm stung from his touch. No, please, God, no! she prayed; she did not want to feel again. Not ever... On leaden feet she walked along the deck and into the main cabin; collapsing on a softly upholstered sofa, she folded her arms defensively across her chest, and was not aware that she was rubbing the elbow he had touched with her hand.

She heard the heavy throb of the engine. She felt the motion of the boat. Not long now and she would be on a flight back to England, she told herself optimistically; then the hair on the back of her neck prickled. She turned her head.

Alex was standing blocking the door, his raw physical presence somehow filling the room. He was watching her with narrowed eyes, his expression unreadable, yet the menace, the iron will behind the impassive face warned that this man was not used to being thwarted by anyone, and certainly not by a woman—especially his wife!

Saffron swallowed nervously. 'What time do we arrive?' she asked—anything to break the fraught silence.

'We already have.' And in a voice as cold and calm as the Arctic he continued, 'We have a deal, you and I—my money for your body and a child; nothing has changed except that I intend to keep you on the yacht until you have fulfilled your part of the bargain.'

She had once compared him to a pirate, and looking at him now, standing barring the door, rock-solid and indomitable, she knew she had been right. 'I don't believe this!' she murmured softly, shaking her head.

'Believe it; you have no choice.'

'Do you honestly expect me to stay with you after last night?' He kept a mistress in Athens and he actually thought he could wield his power and money to pressure her into accepting his infidelity and carrying on as his wife. He was insane!

'You should be grateful it was your lover I punched out. I've never hit a woman in my life, but last night I came pretty close.' His lips twisted in a cynical parody of a smile. 'I blame myself; usually when I make a contract I'm meticulously thorough. In our deal I forgot to stipulate fidelity—an oversight on my part, but one you will never get another chance to exploit.'

Saffron stared at him white-faced, but deep inside the numbness that had encased her for the past few hours was melting and fury was growing, a smouldering anger fed by pain at his betrayal, a pain so sharp that she struggled to breathe. The two-faced, arrogant swine! she thought.

Suddenly her temper snapped. In a blue fury she got to her feet and covered the space between them in a flash, her small hand curved in a fist aimed straight at his jaw.

His hand fastened on her wrist, and her knuckles harmlessly brushed his cheek as he forced her arm behind her back, hauling her tightly against his hard body. 'You little hellion,' he grated between his teeth. 'I'll show you.'

But Saffron was past caring what he said or did. 'You forgot fidelity!' she screeched. 'Don't make me laugh! I know! Do you hear me? I know, you two-timing, sanctimonious pig! James was never my lover, never; I went to him for help after finding your bloody mistress living in your apartment.'

She was free so suddenly that she stumbled back. His hands caught her shoulders to steady her, and his black eyes fastened on her flushed and furious face with a puzzling intensity. 'You went to the apartment last night? What for?' he demanded.

'Not to find Sylvia, that's for sure,' she shot back scathingly.

His grip tightened for a second then relaxed. 'You were looking for me.' An intensely speculative look gleamed in his dark eyes. 'And you found Sylvia.' His hands kneaded her slender shoulders. 'You were jealous.' A hint of a smile curled his lips. 'You were jealous and furious and ran out into the rain, and that's when you sought out James,' he surmised triumphantly, his eyes never leaving her face. 'Have I got it right?'

He was far too astute; he saw far too much, Saffron thought bitterly. 'Bully for you—a regular Sherlock Holmes, no less.' She shrugged. 'So what? It doesn't matter any more.'

'No?' he queried softly. 'I think it does. I think you and I need to talk.'

'We have nothing to talk about. It's over,' she snapped back, and at that moment the yacht hit a large wave and Saffron fell forward hard against him; she felt his body tense to keep their balance, and suddenly she was swept up in his arms and he was striding purposefully across the room and up the gangway to his stateroom.

'Put me down,' she commanded, but she instinctively curved her arm around his neck to prevent herself falling and the numbness that had cushioned her for the past few hours melted completely, an electric awareness jolting through her body. His face so near to hers, the subtle male scent of him, the steady rhythm of his heartbeat were so achingly familiar; she loved the man, and the hurt he had caused her was like a knife shredding her heart.

Alex opened the door and backed into his cabin still holding her. 'Please let me go,' she pleaded, and she meant for good. She could stand no more pain; her emotions were raw, her pride in tatters.

'Never, Saffron,' Alex murmured, and he lowered her slowly down his long body, but kept his arms firmly around her.

She was trapped. She tried to wriggle free, and gasped as she felt the telling stirring of his arousal against her belly. With one hand he stroked up her back and tangled his fingers in her hair, forcing her to look up into his dark, brooding face.

'Sex is no solution,' she said, recognising the deepening gleam in his brown eyes and determined not to give in to his potent masculine appeal, even as her body ached to do so.

'No, but love is!'

'What would you know about love? You've had more women than hot dinners—a mistress, a wife—even your own mother is frightened of you!' Saffron lashed back, staring up at him with unconcealed belligerence. He had the nerve to mention love to her! He didn't know the meaning of the word. His wealth and looks, his confidence and power assured that he always had a willing woman in his bed. He didn't need love, didn't understand the concept. And she had been an idiot to imagine for a moment that she could change him.

'I love you.' He smiled without humour. 'Though I don't expect you to believe me.'

Saffron blinked. Had she heard right? Her eyes flashed up, wide and wondering. He avoided her gaze, his long lashes shielding his eyes but not quite masking the unfamiliar vulnerability in their black depths.

'I know I've treated you badly, but you must listen. Allow me to speak in my own defence.' And with a quick return to his usual self he pinned her with a look of arrogant authority. 'You're my wife—you owe me that much.'

Intrigued, and with a glimmer of hope in her shattered heart, Saffron said, 'So talk.'

'Can we sit down first?' he asked, and she allowed him to lead her to the bed. They sat side by side, not touching.

'When I first met you, you attacked me, infuriated me and entranced me all at the same time. I thought I was too old for love, didn't really believe in it. I told myself it was simply sex, a fierce chemical reaction whenever I was near you. I was determined to have you in my bed.'

'I remember.' Saffron smiled slightly as the image of a near-naked Alex the first morning on the yacht rose up to tempt her.

'Yes. Well.' Alex turned slightly and, lifting his hand, brushed a few golden curls from her brow. 'A red headed vision of loveliness, you fascinated me so much that I didn't care if you were another of my mother's traps. In my conceit I thought it was only a matter of time before you fell into my arms. But you proved me wrong.'

If only he knew, she thought, that from the first day she'd been aching for him. She lowered her eyes, her gaze fixed on her hands clasped in her lap. 'A first for you, no doubt,' she said with a tinge of sarcasm. She wanted to believe him, but . . .

'Damn it, look at me, Saffron!' The forceful command surprised her, and her eyes flashed to his as he grasped both her hands in his much larger ones. 'Cut the sarcasm and give me a chance. Give us a chance.'

'Us'. His voice was persuasive, deep and soft as velvet. She looked at him and oh, how she wanted to trust him!

'You were a first for me, a woman who wasn't mine for the taking. I had never had that trouble before. I'm a wealthy man; women fall over themselves for my money, and I thought you would be the same.'

'You believe I am the same,' Saffron could not help inserting. 'Your deal said as much.'

Alex turned her hands over in his, his thumbs rubbing her palms, sending tremors of delight through her. 'I said a lot of things I didn't mean.' He raised his dark eyes to her face. 'But you drove me to it, Saffron. When you left Greece for London, I told myself it didn't matter, I would see you again, but the very next day I was telephoning you. I missed you. But I was still not prepared to admit it was anything more than sex, even when I followed you to London and took you out to dinner and back to my apartment. It was only when you walked out that night after demanding marriage that I began to worry.'

'You, worry?' Saffron could not imagine anything bothering the indomitable Alex.

'Yes; I'm as human as the next man. Very human,' he husked, and, lifting her hands, he pressed a kiss on each palm.

'No. You said talk; the truth.' Saffron knew they had to get everything out in the open; there could be no secrets between them if their marriage was to have any chance at all.

'Yes.' He smiled grimly. 'The truth. I spent a sleepless night, and convinced myself marriage was a good idea. A good deal. I was nearly forty, it was time I thought of an heir, it would make my mother happy, and I got you in my bed. I refused to admit to myself it was anything more. Even when I proposed the next day I was still deluding myself.'

Saffron knew all about delusions; hadn't she suffered from the same virus, with her stupid plot for revenge? 'Alex...'

'Let me finish, Saffron—now, while I have the nerve. I spent all last night preparing this speech and I have to do it.'

This was an Alex she had never seen before—her all-powerful husband was uncertain, nervous, even contrite! 'Go on,' she prompted softly.

'On our wedding-day, putting the ring on your finger, I was exultant. Arrogantly I congratulated myself on having got the girl I wanted, desired above all others, without having to admit I was in love. I couldn't wait to get you alone in Paris. But my devious desire backfired spectacularly on our wedding night when you told me the reason behind your demand for marriage.'

She gazed up at his sombre face and saw the lingering trace of remembered pain in the depths of his dark eyes. How could they have got it so wrong? she asked herself, moisture glazing her eyes. 'I accused you of being little better than a pimp,' she said with a regretful shake of her head.

'I could have killed you then.' Alex's eyes flashed briefly with remembered anger. 'That the woman I was finally beginning to realise I loved could think so badly of me, that I could be so easily deceived only proved what I had always known: love made one vulnerable and was to be avoided at all costs. But I couldn't let you go, I wanted you too much, so I suggested our bargain.'

'Suggested? Ordered more like,' Saffron corrected him, then lifted her hand from his and reached up to stroke her slender fingers down his hard cheek. He had said he loved her again. Perhaps it was her turn to be brave and take a chance, try to explain.

'I confessed the truth on our wedding night not because I wanted revenge, but simply because I knew I loved you, and I couldn't go through with a marriage made for all the wrong reasons. I think I secretly hoped that if I could forgive the fact that you owned the club that destroyed Eve and you could forgive my stupid bid for revenge then maybe we could start again.'

'You loved me then?' Alex queried in amazement. 'Enough to think that badly of me and still forgive me?' His voice was hoarse and, slipping an arm around her narrow shoulders, his free hand covering hers where it rested on his cheek, he continued, 'You humble me with your love and compassion, Saffron, and to think I repaid you by making love to you on our wedding night in anger. Hurting you, destroying your love. I'm sorry.'

'Don't be.' Safe in his arms with his avowal of love echoing in her heart, she freely confessed, 'You didn't hurt me; it was the most wonderful experience of my life. I enjoyed it.'

'That has been part of my trouble,' Alex said ruefully. 'I enjoy you too much. I've never known or imagined a woman like you. In my arms, in our bed, you're so beautiful, so passionately responsive, you make me lose all control. It frightens me.'

'It's the same for me,' Saffron murmured.

'But don't you see?' he swept on. 'Because sex between us was so fantastic, when I got you on

Serendipidos, in my conceit, I smugly concluded that our deal was perfect and much better than mushy avowals of love. You were great friends with my mother and I was your first and only lover; there was no way you would leave me.'

'Modesty becomes you,' she said drily.

His smile was wry as he lowered his head and kissed her softly. 'Jackass springs to mind,' he derided himself, before adding in a much more serious tone, 'But last night, seeing you in James's apartment, I was knocked right off my axis, my supreme arrogance destroyed. By sheer chance I had called there, and to find my half-naked wife coming out of the bathroom...' He shook his head as if to banish the image.

Quick to reassure him, Saffron said, 'Nothing happened, Alex; I arrived half an hour before you, soaked to the skin and in tears. I asked James to arrange for me to return to England immediately. Instead he gave me a stiff drink and told me to get out of my wet clothes and then we could talk. You know the rest.'

'God, yes! I saw red and hit him, but even in my rage the worst part, the thing that ripped my pride to shreds, was the fact that I never for a second considered letting you go. I didn't care if he was your lover.' His dark gaze burned into hers as he amended quickly, 'No, I did care, I was absolutely gutted, but there was no way in the world I could live without you. Never to have you in my arms again, to bury myself deep in your feminine softness... Ego, pride, you could trample on the lot and I still couldn't let you go. I love you...'

Saffron's eyes widened. She had longed for his love for so long and had tried to believe that it was possible. But she hadn't dared hope for anything like this. Her dynamic, powerful husband was laying his heart at her feet. She leant towards him. 'I lo——' But she stopped

as the reason for her distress the previous evening came
back to taunt her.

Alex, sensing her hesitation, pulled her up and on to
his lap, his arms tightening fiercely around her. 'You
don't have to say you love me. Not now. I simply want
the chance to win your love.' His dark eyes searched her
beautiful but wary face. 'I will in the end; I'm a determined man and I'll never give up, supposing it takes a
lifetime.' His hand slipped beneath her shirt and stroked
up her back while his other hand caught her chin and
turned her face to his. 'How can I persuade you to take
a chance on me?'

'I went to Athens yesterday to surprise you, and hopefully talk you into letting me go back to work.' Saffron
burst into speech, refusing to give in to the seductive
trail of his hand on her bare back. 'The island is quiet
in the winter; I was feeling lonely and it seemed a good
idea at the time—until I went to the apartment and discovered you shared it with Sylvia.'

All his protestations of love faded against the incon-
trovertible truth, Saffron realised sadly. Sylvia was his
mistress. She had seen it with her own eyes on this very
yacht, outside this very cabin, never mind last night.

She attempted to slide off his lap but with easy strength
Alex held her close and, falling back on the bed within
seconds, she was flat on her back, Alex leaning over her,
his lower body imprisoning hers while his hands rested
either side of her head.

'It's no good denying it, Alex. I saw your clothes next
to hers in the wardrobe.'

'Saffron, darling, I'm flattered by your jealousy but
I swear I have never, ever made love to Sylvia. In fact
I have never so much as looked at another woman since
the moment I saw you. A few of my clothes may still
be in the wardrobe, but I have never stayed there with

Sylvia or any other woman. I offered Sylvia the use of the apartment for the rest of her stay in Greece simply because she told me she was tired of living in a hotel, and as it was my fault she had to stay here to oversee the selling of the health club chain I thought it was the least I could do. I moved out to a hotel.

'In a way it was your fault. I'm off-loading the health clubs so you can't possibly think, even for a second, I would be involved in anything so seedy as a massage parlour.' He grinned cheekily. 'Anyway, I hope to keep my own personal masseuse.'

Saffron was stunned by his action but still found it hard to forget Sylvia so easily.

Seeing the uncertainty in her eyes, Alex lowered his head, his hard mouth brushing gently over her brow, down her nose and finally touching her lips. 'Think, Saffron. We have never spent a night apart since Aunt Katherina revealed I was not the villain you thought.'

He was right but she still wasn't convinced. 'Alex, I know you and Sylvia were once lovers.'

'Rubbish.' He bit the tip of her chin gently. 'Forget Sylvia; I love you and right now I want you quite desperately.'

Saffron sighed softly, her pulse speeding as Alex moved his long legs either side of hers, allowing her to feel his urgency. 'When we were cruising I saw Sylvia leaving your cabin early one morning,' she got out breathlessly.

Alex reared back. 'Never.'

'Don't lie to me, Alex. I walked into the hall one morning and Sylvia was leaving your cabin.'

'Saffron, I swear to you she had not spent the night with me. For God's sake, you know I spent the whole of the cruise trying to get you into bed; how could I look at another woman?'

That much was true, Saffron allowed.

'I don't know why the damned woman was at my door, but I'm telling you the truth.' His dark eyes bored down into hers, his expression grim. 'Sylvia's leaving my employ next week, she's going to work for the new owners, but before she does I'm damn well going to get to the bottom of this.' He rolled on to his side and sat up, shoving his hand distractedly through his black hair. 'I don't know how to convince you, but I will,' he said adamantly, with a swift return to his usual masculine arrogance.

Saffron tried to sit up, but he shoved her back among the pillows. She saw his shoulders coming near, the determined light in his black eyes, and she lifted her hands to his chest in an effort to restrain him. She refused to let him convince her with sex. It was too important.

'Saffron?' he rasped in query.

She looked at him, his jutting chin, the firm line of his jaw, and she almost believed him, wanted to give in to the promise in his eyes. But she remembered just how hard and insensitive he could be, even resorting to violence with James.

'Your own mother told me you always took one or more of your women on the family cruise.' And, determined to air all her grievances, Saffron added, 'And she didn't dare tell you that your father loved Aunt Katherina.'

She stopped. She should not have said that; she knew Anna had a great ability to be economical with the truth. She waited, holding her breath, expecting Alex to explode, but instead, to her absolute amazement, he threw his head back and laughed out loud.

'My God, I should have guessed; dear, demented Mother.' And, gathering her in his arms, he rolled across the bed, swinging her on top of him.

Sprawled across his hot, hard body, his arms tightening around her, she could only gasp, 'Demented?' Alex was the only demented person around here, she thought as he continued to laugh.

'Saffron, my sweet, naïve Saffron,' he teased, and she glared down at him, only to be rewarded with a swift kiss on her full lips. 'Surely you've realised by now that my mother is the original drama queen?'

'Drama queen?' she murmured. Alex's amusement and the surge of desire that went through her at his kiss and his hand stroking up and down her back as she lay against him, were hazing her brain.

'My mother, much as I love her, can't help herself,' Alex said, and, finally controlling his amusement, he continued, 'She was a dancer when she met my father but her ambition was to be an actress. My father worshipped the ground she walked on, and if anything was far too indulgent. He listened to her dramatic stories put up with her trips to London for the theatre, the opera, the art.

'She probably told you the old story of Aunt Katherina and my father; it was nothing. Katherina dated my father twice, met his brother and that was it, but Mama liked to embroider the truth; she can't help herself. I should have stopped her years ago, but, like my father, I tend to indulge her. I was eighteen when I had to take over the running of the family, and I can tell you that looking after three women—my mother, aunt and cousin—is no joke; I would rather run a multinational business any day.'

Saffron believed him. Hadn't she been puzzled by the easy friendship of the two women on Serendipidos? 'The chopstick poet,' she murmured.

'Exactly; that sounds like Mama.' An affectionate smile curved Alex's mouth. 'You can't believe half she tells you, and the rest is usually a vast exaggeration. But I love her.' His voice thickened as his hand slipped under the waistband of her jeans, curving her bare bottom. 'And I love you, quite desperately, Saffron. Believe me.'

She did... It was in character, Saffron realised, for Alex to allow Sylvia the use of the apartment. He had been taking care of women all his life, and, thinking back to the morning on the yacht, she had not actually seen Sylvia leave his cabin; she had been standing with her hand on the door. In that moment Saffron acknowledged that there were some things she would have to take on trust. The decision made, she smiled, a wide, beauteous curve of her full lips.

'I do believe you, Alex, and I do love you,' she said simply, her green eyes, soft and full of emotion, gazing down on his darkly handsome face. Tomorrow, she would use that test and, God willing, she would be able to give him the greatest gift of love—a child.

'Saffron, my darling,' Alex husked, pulling her head down to his and kissing her with all the urgency and pent-up emotion of a man starved of love for years, instead of only one night.

Clothes were discarded in frantic haste as they rolled around the wide bed in a tangle of arms and legs, mouth seeking mouth, hands touching, caressing, teasing, tormenting, until finally Saffron lay beneath her husband's taut, poised body, shaking on the brink of completion. 'Please, Alex,' she pleaded. 'Now.'

Alex raised his head, his eyes glowing with an incredible warmth and passion as his broad chest rubbed over the throbbing fullness of her breasts. 'Now——' He joined with her. 'Now and forever I will love you, in this world and through all eternity,' he declared thickly as finally he moved slowly and deeply, his great body claiming her, fulfilling her wildest dreams.

Coming Next Month

HARLEQUIN PRESENTS®

THE BEST HAS JUST GOTTEN BETTER

#1833 THE FATHER OF HER CHILD Emma Darcy
Lauren didn't want to fall in love again—but when she saw
Michael all her good resolutions went out the window. And
when she learned he was out to break her heart she vowed
never to see him again. But it was too late....

#1834 WILD HUNGER Charlotte Lamb
Book Four: *SINS*
Why was Gerard, famous foreign correspondent, following
Keira? She could hardly believe he was interested in the story of
a supermodel fighting a constant battle with food. No, he want-
ed something more....

#1835 THE TROPHY HUSBAND Lynne Graham
(9 to 5)
When Sara caught her fiancé being unfaithful, her boss, Alex,
helped pick up the pieces of her life. But Sara wondered what
price she would have to pay for his unprecedented kindness.

#1836 THE STRENGTH OF DESIRE Alison Fraser
(This Time, Forever)
The death of Hope's husband brought his brother, Guy, back
into her life, and left her with two legacies. Both meant that
neither Hope nor Guy would be able to forget their erstwhile
short-lived affair.

#1837 FRANCESCA Sally Wentworth
(Ties of Passion, 2)
Francesca was used to having the best of everything—and that
included men. The uncouth Sam was a far cry from her usual
boyfriends, but he was the only man who had ever loved her for
what she was rather than what she had.

#1838 TERMS OF POSSESSION Elizabeth Power
Nadine needed money—and Cameron needed a child. His offer
was extraordinary—he would possess her body and soul and
the resulting baby would be his. But the arrangements were
becoming complicated...

HARLEQUIN PRESENTS®

PRIVATE & CONFIDENTIAL

MEMO

To: The Reader

From: The Editor at Harlequin Presents

Subject: —our six sizzling stories of office romance!

When Sara caught her fiancé being unfaithful, Alex, her boss, helped pick up the pieces of her life. But Sara wondered what price she would have to pay for his unexpected kindness....

P.S.#1835 THE TROPHY HUSBAND
by Lynne Graham

P.P.S. Available in September wherever Harlequin books are sold.

Look us up on-line at: http://www.romance.net

HARLEQUIN PRESENTS®

**brings you the best books
by the best authors!**

EMMA DARCY
Award-winning author
"Pulls no punches..."   —*Romantic Times*

Watch for:
#1833 The Father of Her Child
by Emma Darcy

Lauren didn't want to fall in love again—but
when she saw Michael all her good resolutions
went out the window....

Harlequin Presents—the best has just gotten better!
Available in September wherever
Harlequin books are sold.

TAUTH-12

HARLEQUIN PRESENTS®

Ties of Passion
by Sally Wentworth

The story of the Brodey family. Money, looks, style—the
Brodeys have everything...except love.

Read part one of this exciting three-part series

#1832 CHRIS

Chris Brodey could offer Tiffany anything she wanted,
but she soon discovered that he wasn't a man prepared to
give something for nothing....

Watch for books two and three in
September and October!

Available in August wherever Harlequin books are sold.

 HARLEQUIN PRESENTS®

Love can conquer the deadliest of !

Indulge in Charlotte Lamb's exciting seven-part series

Watch for:

The Sin of Gluttony
in

#1834 WILD HUNGER

Why was Gerard, the famous journalist, following Keira?
She could hardly believe he was interested in the story of
a supermodel fighting a battle with food....